HUNTING FOR AVERY (POLICE AND FIRE: OPERATION ALPHA)

ECP - BRAVO MANHUNTERS, BOOK 5

ANNIE MILLER

Dear Readers,

Welcome to the Police and Fire: Operation Alpha Fan-Fiction world!

If you are new to this amazing world, in a nutshell the author wrote a story using one or more of my characters in it. Sometimes that character has a major role in the story, and other times they are only mentioned briefly. This is perfectly legal and allowable because they are going through Aces Press to publish the story.

This book is entirely the work of the author who wrote it. While I might have assisted with brainstorming and other ideas about which of my characters to use, I didn't have any part in the process or writing or editing the story.

I'm proud and excited that so many authors loved my characters enough that they wanted to write them into their own story. Thank you for supporting them, and me!

READ ON!
    Xoxo
    Susan Stoker

Our todays and yesterdays are what lead us into our tomorrows. May we never look back and wish we could've changed the past, because it's our past that will pave our future.

PROLOGUE

Jared chuckled as he listened to the reporter. Should he count her as one or two victims? He hadn't known she was pregnant, not that it would've stopped him. She'd already been in his sights. Jared had thought she was fat, but he wasn't picky, unlike most. He'd target fat or skinny, white or black, short or tall. The only ones he shied away from were the elderly. Not that he cared about them, because he didn't. It was because they were too weak to fight, and he loved fighters. Even now he got excited remembering the woman begging for him to not hurt her. "I'm having a baby. Please don't." Only Jared did, he always did.

It was time to pull up the news report online. The printout would be placed right beside the other seven. Again, would she be number eight and nine? He'd think about it. He wondered what the police thought. Grinning, Jared took the printed news report and read it out loud, relishing at hearing his own voice as he read about the victim.

"Texas native Hillary Phelan, thirty-one, became the eighth victim of the River Walk Strangler. Some would say her unborn child was the ninth victim…" So, they did count

1

it as two kills. Grinning at his accomplishment, Jared continued to read.

"The local FBI office has issued a formal statement indicating a joint investigation with the Texas Rangers. Click below to see the news conference."

Hovering his mouse over the link, he watched as the FBI Agent and the Ranger stood side by side at the podium.

"The FBI and Texas Rangers have come up with a profile of the murderer. He's a highly educated white male, between thirty and forty years old. He's patient, but also an opportunist, as none of his victims are related or bear any similarities."

"Special Agent Cruz," a voice called out.

When the cameraman scanned the crowd, he saw the cute brunette jumping up and down waving her microphone in the air. As if realizing she'd gained their attention, she began her interrogation.

"Agent Cruz, the last victim was pregnant and wasn't discovered at the River Walk. Why do you believe she was the strangler's victim?"

"Ms. Andrews, this is an open case, and I will not speak of the specifics, but based on our findings, Hillary Phelan and her unborn child were murdered by the man the media has dubbed the River Walk Strangler."

Another reporter picked up the conversation with his own line of questions.

"Are the police and FBI holding back any pertinent information that might protect San Antonio residents?"

The tall and intimidating Texas Ranger, Dax something, walked up to the microphone.

"You know better than that, Bill. Our entire goal is to catch this murderer, bring justice to the families of his victims, and protect all of our citizens from senseless crimes and violence."

He watched as the Ranger straightened his bolo tie and walked off the stage. His stance made it clear he was unhappy.

"I will answer one more question," Cruz announced over the muttering crowd.

"The last victim's husband is in the Army, stationed in Killeen. Has he been notified of his family's murder?"

"We have notified his Commanding Officer. We ask that you respect our brave soldier, and respect that he's received a double blow with the loss of his wife and child."

Jared watched as the FBI agent followed the Ranger and exited the stage, clearly uncomfortable with the last line of questioning. "Who are you, Joe Phelan?"

He didn't know, but he would by the end of the day. Jared looked forward to getting to know more about the active soldier. What would he do when he discovered he'd lost everything in one quick strangulation? Would the Feds tell him about the little treat he'd left the man? Would they show him a picture of his handiwork? Would the image of his little boy resting on his mother's chest be the image that would haunt him for the rest of his life?

Jared closed the web browser, secured the news article alongside his polaroid pictures, and the umbilical cord of the child who never had a chance to take his first breath.

* * *

"Sergeant First Class Phelan, how do you plead to the Section 934, Article 134 charge of assault with intent to kill?"

"Not Guilty."

"Sergeant First Class Phelan, how do you plead to the Section 928, Article 128 charge of assault consummated by a battery?"

"Guilty."

"Sergeant First Class Phelan, how do you plead to the Section 928a, Article 128a charge of intent of permanently maiming military personnel?"

"Not Guilty."

"Sergeant First Class Phelan, how do you plead to the Section 933, Article 133 charge of misconduct unbecoming an officer?"

"Guilty."

"Sergeant First Class Phelan, how do you plead to the Section 917, Article 117 charge of provoking speech and gestures? "

"Guilty."

"Sergeant First Class Phelan, how do you plead to the Section 915, Article 115 charge of communicating threats, generally speaking?"

"Guilty."

"Sergeant First Class Phelan, the members of this court have no doubt that the underlying reasoning for your outburst and violence was a reaction to news that your wife and child were murdered. We've looked for any opportunity for leniency, however two factors weigh heavily against this. First, you are a member of covert Special Operations. As a team member of Delta Force, your judgment must be clear at all times. It is unacceptable to lose your temper in such a way to physically assault another serviceman, and especially not your Commanding Officer. The second reason is because you yourself have acknowledged your wrongdoing by pleading guilty to four counts of wrongful misconduct. Collectively, your guilty charges equate to five years, if served consecutively, however the members agree that you will serve all four counts concurrently, with the Article 128 three years incarceration being the prison sentence at Leavenworth. This sentence also strips you of all military awards and merits. You will also forfeit all pay and allowances, including all benefits granted to a military serviceman. This charge also requires you be discharged without honor at the end of your time served. Do you understand the sentencing and its implications?"

"Yes, sir."

"Is there anything you'd like to say to the members of this court?"

"Yes, sir." Bench turned to the eight members and saluted them collectively. "Gentleman and Ladies, I am proud to have served this great nation, and I'm sorry if my behavior has brought reproach and shame to my Delta team or the Army. However, I loved my wife and the child we weren't able to hold in our arms. When I discovered my wife's death and burial happened while I was on a mission, well, as you know I lost it, but I don't regret my reaction. I may not have been able to save my family, but I should've been able to say my goodbyes. I humbly and willingly accept my sentencing." At the end of his speech, he saluted the members once more and extended his arms out for the required handcuffing.

Bench didn't miss the tears falling from the members of his jury. Nor did he salute his Commanding Officer, who not only chose to keep his wife's murder and funeral from him until the mission was complete; but who maliciously claimed murder was his intent. Everyone knows the training a Delta operative has, if Bench had wanted the CO dead, he would be. As he was led out of the courtroom, he looked at his former CO, who had ruined his own career in the public eye, and winked. Bench would pay his dues, then he'd discover a life after losing everything that was important to him; his family and the military.

PART I

CHAPTER 1

Another rejection letter.

Avery put it in the ever-bulging manilla folder. It would rest comfortably with the other sixteen letters.

They all seemed to begin the same way,

Ms. Grey,

'We appreciate your interest in publishing with (insert name here). We love hearing from authors and their passion for their manuscripts. However, as enjoyable as the read was, it's not something we're looking for at this time. We wish you the very best in your endeavors. Please reach out to... blah, blah, blah.'

This was what her professor would've called a reconstructed sandwich, soft, hard, then soft again. In all reality, the letter sounded more like Charlie Brown's teacher, Miss Othmar... wah-wah-wah-wah-wah.

But Avery wouldn't be dismissed. She'd made the decision to be a writer, and knew what it entailed... long hours, mental fatigue, mood swings, and the ever present feeling of rejection. She could go from exhilaration to disappointment with a click of the mouse.

Fortunately, Avery's English Lit professor took a liking to

her. Without Professor Angelakos and his leads, she would have had a hard time paying rent some months.

One thing she knew for sure, she wouldn't ask her parents for help. She took pride in being a thirty-something who paid her own way, albeit on a shoestring budget.

When she told her parents about her career choice, her mother sighed, as if she'd told them she was going to strip for money. Ironically, her father would have approved of that profession. She loved her parents, but they were boring. She couldn't remember the last time they varied their schedule, or took a trip that went beyond the border of Texas, much less to someplace exotic like Europe.

She'd once told her parents about one of her articles being published in the San Antonio Express News, she'd expected something a little more enthusiastic than, 'That's nice, Avery Marie.'

Her parents called her by her first and middle name. She wasn't one of those kids who knew they were in trouble when their full name was used. No, Avery's parents believed if they took the time to give her a middle name, then it only made sense that they used it. On the flipside, they were rarely angry with her, but they could hand out disappointment like candy on Halloween.

She could list their disappointments just as quickly as she could say her full name.

First, her career choice. Yes, writing was a career. She'd barely eked out a little over minimum wage, but she loved what she did. Wasn't that worth more than dollars and cents? Answer... Not according to her landlord.

Second, when she walked away from Jeffery. Her only regret was saying yes to him. Yes to a first date. Yes to a second one, and especially yes to his marriage proposal. At the time Avery hadn't been familiar with the term gaslighting, but her relationship with Jeffery was textbook.

He always found some kind of fault with her, and then waited for her to apologize for he saw as incompetence. She was too fat, so she went of a diet. She was too messy, so she cleaned her house as if she had OCD. She supposedly interrogated him, so she kept her questions and opinions to herself. She'd had enough, and ended their engagement. She knew it was the right thing to do, and didn't regret making the decision. Unfortunately, her family thought she'd lost her mind.

Third, she didn't compare to her brother. Oh, she loved Tim. He'd been her champion growing up. She knew he'd always have her back, but then he left for college. After that, there was no buffer between her and her parents. Unfortunately, she couldn't avoid being in their line of fire. All their attention caused her to have anxiety problems. The feeling of suffocation and claustrophobia were part of the reasons why she'd never invested in finding someone to love. She'd seen firsthand the results of having someone controlling in your life.

Then Tim came home with a girlfriend, who later became his wife. Melissa was a perfect fit with the Grey family, which only magnified her parent's disappointment in Avery. There were times Avery felt her parents preferred Melissa to herself. And on some base level, she agreed.

Equipped with his criminal justice degree, Tim worked his way to becoming a Texas Ranger, and wore the white hat well.

Even though Tim's job came with danger, her parents supported it. In fact, they boasted about their son, the Ranger. When friends asked about Avery's career, she'd only heard them say, *'she's still figuring it out.'*

The last way she'd failed her parents was when Tim and Melissa gave them grandchildren. Her mother's snide remarks about throwing her future away became more

11

frequent, to the point that her mother suggested she apologize to Jeffery so he'd take her back.

"After he sees how sorry you are, you can get married. We still have your wedding dress," her mother said one night after a Grey family dinner.

"We were hoping you'd come to your senses and stop being foolish," her father added.

"Of course, we'd have to have it altered." Avery's mother had been harping on her gaining weight after the botched wedding.

"I can finally eat again. I don't have someone telling me to watch my weight, or criticize me when I order a slice of lemon pie."

"He wanted you well. He knows the risks obesity can have on a body. He is a doctor after all."

"Good grief, Mom. You'd think he was a brain surgeon the way you talk about him. He's an ears, nose, and throat doctor. I'm not saying that's not impressive, it's just unlikely he knows the effects, since ears can't get fat."

If only those had been isolated conversations, but they were occurring weekly, sometimes twice a week.

Looking at the rejection letter, she once again owed her professor a huge thanks. The opportunity he'd recommended her for was exactly what she needed to move her career forward. Writing with this famous author could open doors that she'd never been able to push through. If she was hired, she could use the pearls of wisdom this author surely had to offer and become the author she knew was lying just below the surface.

* * *

"Mr. Easton, I can't tell you how great it is to meet you," Avery said after she'd shaken the hand of both New York Times and USA Today's bestseller Callum Easton.

"Callum, please. We're going to be working with each other for the next few months, so please call me Callum or Easton. I've been called a lot worse."

Avery sat across from a beautiful man... and beautiful was the right description. He was scholarly looking, almost nerdy. Not that she cared. It was his career and her own possibilities that she concentrated on. But she wasn't stupid enough not to see the man for what he was... beautiful. He had beautiful amber-colored eyes and unbelievably long lashes. He had dimples when he smiled. Really, who didn't like dimples? But no matter how beautiful he was... he was married, and she didn't flirt with someone else's man, nor ignore the risks of dating a co-worker. She learned that lesson a little too easily.

"Angelakos had nothing but great things to say about you."

"I love him. I think I would've gone for my masters and even a PhD if I could've taken only his classes. He's amazing."

Avery wanted to have a redo, a mulligan, anything to erase and restart the conversation. How could Callum take her as a serious writer when all of her adjectives were so pedestrian? Beautiful, amazing, great... ugh... cue in the faceplant here.

"He is that. I agree that his classes were the most insightful."

'See? He uses better adjectives. Idiot.'

"This is my first-time ghostwriting for someone. Can you tell me what you're looking for?"

"Yes, of course. I've used a ghostwriter once before, but she wasn't amenable to making changes to her draft, so it became a hostile work environment. I wasn't going to hire another assistant, but Angelakos recommended you. He emailed me a couple of excerpts from your assignments, and I was impressed. So, I'm relying heavily on the Professor's recommendation."

"I appreciate that."

"Some ghostwriters write the entire book, then it's published under the client's name."

"Oh. Okay." She wasn't sure if she wanted to write the entire novel and receive no recognition. How was this process beneficial to the writer?

"However, that's not how I work. I'm looking for a collaborator. This is a non-fiction project, and it will require a massive amount of research."

"So more researching than writing?"

"Not exactly, I have a lot of research already done. When I'm writing a novel, I usually end up with too much information. I have to trim and cut it down so I'm not lecturing the reader. However, that research, can be useful for other books. That's the case with this novel. We're looking at what makes a copycat so invested in the original. For example, the River Walk Strangler. Jared Ramsey was caught by accident. The police didn't have a real lead even after nine murders. Was Mr. Ramsey looking to round out the number to ten or would he have ever stopped? That's not something we know because he's never agreed to an interview until now."

"He's going to meet with you?"

"No, he's going to meet with *you*. But here's where the collaboration comes in. You and I will make a draft of what we want to know; which questions to ask, and what we hope to gain from the interview. Then you'll write a draft. We'll review your notes and see what's still missing from the first draft."

"Are we only looking at the River Walk Strangler?"

"Not necessarily. Of course, we'll know more once you interview him. If we gain nothing useful, we'll move on to another serial killer. I'd like to concentrate on Ramsey since he's local, and now has an active copycat. I'm hopeful we can pick up some useful data."

"I'm guessing I'll also be speaking with the police who handled the case?"

"Yes, that's part of the research. You'll find a lot of information on Google, but if that's all we were going to do, why write a book at all?"

"That makes sense."

"Avery, think of your job as an investigative reporter. You'll dig up everything you can, then ask all the right questions in your interview with Ramsey. That means you'll be looking at any possible leads. What, if anything, was missed by the FBI and Rangers? Interview the victim's families. There's a lot of research that I haven't done... hands on type of research."

"I can do this. My brother always told me I was nosy. And I've always asked why about everything I learned."

"That's exactly what I'm looking for. For the time being, you should send over your interview notes and first draft. I'll review it, then we'll meet and discuss any changes I have. I'd expect we'll have three drafts before we're ready for proofreading and editing."

"Do you have a deadline?"

"My publisher has me on a pretty tight turnaround. I'll need your first draft in two weeks. I'm hoping that will give you enough time to speak with Ramsey, the FBI and the Rangers. I doubt you'll get to the families, but that really depends on how much you can achieve."

"And my fees? How is that paid? By the hour? By the word count?"

"This is where I made serious mistakes with my former

associate. I had paid her upfront, regardless of her making deadlines or taking my notes and comments into consideration. I need someone I can trust with my words, my reputation, and my contacts. So here's my offer. I received an advance from my editor. I will give you half, however in portions. When I receive the first draft and we've reviewed it together, I'll pay you a quarter of the salary. With each draft, you'll receive the next quarter. If it appears we're not on the same page, you will have already been paid for your time invested in research and writing. Fair?"

"More than fair."

When Callum told her what each quarter payout would be, Avery had to close her mouth before she screamed in excitement. Just one quarter would pay her car off. She could pay rent for an entire year with the next quarter. She would make more in one quarter, than she'd ever made collectively from her own writing.

"If you finish before the deadline, and the work is up to my standards, I'll give you two thousand dollars each week you're ahead of schedule."

Avery was doing the math in her head and couldn't stop the head bobbing. She wanted to apologize for her excitement, and she tried to tamp it down. She had to remember she was a professional, or at least she was going to fake it until she made it.

"I'll have my attorney draft it all in writing. You'll have time to have your own attorney review it before we start the collaboration."

"That's perfect." Perfect meant that she'd Google any terminology she didn't understand. Attorney? Yeah right, not unless Janie will do it for free.

"Now for the collaboration. You will not be listed on the cover. The work will be published under my name. You will, however, be listed in the acknowledgment as my researcher."

"That's okay. But how can I use this experience to present to potential literary agents?"

"Unfortunately, you won't be able to. That being said, if I'm happy with your writing, your work ethics, and your ability to listen to criticism, then my agent will be made aware of your input. He's always looking for talented authors and researchers. He will be able to decide how best to use your talents, but that's a conversation for later. But like I said, I'll only make the introductions if I'm one hundred percent satisfied with your work."

"Oh, Callum, this is perfect. I'm sure you remember how difficult it is to break into the literary world. I will do everything I can to ensure you're happy with my research and writing."

"I believe you will. Now, I'll have my attorney reach out to you and get the necessary documents signed. It will entail everything we've talked about today, including the potential introduction to my agent."

They both stood, and Avery had to hold herself back from launching herself at him for a hug. Instead, she shook his hand and left his office with the world's largest grin. For the first time, she had a real chance of turning her passion into a paid career.

'Finally!'

CHAPTER 2

Bench tossed the mail onto the kitchen countertop of his bare apartment. When he'd lived in Killeen, he and Hillary had a rental off base. Their two-bedroom house wasn't large, but it was perfect for them and their impending son. Hillary had a place for everything, and she always complained when he tossed the mail where it didn't belong.

"Joe, if you don't put things in their place, how will we know we've received everything?"

Bench took the mail he'd tossed and began sorting through it. Hillary's voice was always in his head. She generally scolded him from anything like the mail, to his solitary life, and most recently about his MMA fights. He'd never been angry while they were married, he'd only wanted to please her. But from the day he'd learned of her death, the anger had never left.

In prison, he'd spent his time working out. He'd gone into the cell weighing one seventy-five. Special Force operatives weren't generally as buff or ripped as the men he'd seen on the covers of romance novels. Hillary had brought one of those books home one day and asked why he didn't look like the model.

"There's nothing real about that picture. How could he carry a hostage or run twenty miles if his muscles sapped him of his strength?"

"Honey, I'm joking. These guys are just man-candy. I prefer your skinny body."

"Skinny," he smirked and picked her up, tossed her over his shoulder and jogged to their bedroom. "I'll show you that there's nothing skinny about me."

She'd never recognize him now. His body now resembled the eye-candy his wife taunted him with. Even though he'd gained thirty pounds, not one ounce of it was fat. At ECP, he didn't need the same stamina required as a Delta, not that he'd let himself go. Bench had spent time with Bama and Archer, the two tallest men at ECP, sparring in the ring. Bench had to hold some of his punches and kicks, not wanting to let his anger surface. He had to pull back even more when he trained Susan, also known as Doc. He'd wanted her to be able to defend herself. Maybe if he'd taught Hillary some self-defense, he'd have never lost her. He'd spent the last five years living in the world of *what ifs*.

Bench noticed a bank statement. He never opened them, not since the first one. Hillary's life insurance remained untouched in his savings account. His mother told him to put the hundred grand into a CD or IRA, but he wasn't looking to make money off of the deposit. Even the fifty-bucks it earned each year while sitting in the account was too much.

Behind the bank statement was another letter from him. Why did Jared continue writing him? He didn't have to ask, he knew. Hillary and their son had been his last victims. In the first letter, he'd vividly detailed how he killed her, how he cut his son out of his mother's womb, and the souvenir he'd kept.

When he confronted the Texas Ranger about the umbilical cord, they'd admitted to keeping that information from the public. Only Bench wasn't the public. It had been a link that bound his wife and son together, and now it was in the hands of a sick and deranged man.

Those early days had been the worst. Hillary's family was hurt and mad that he hadn't come home when it happened. It took a lot to convince them that he hadn't known. His conviction and prison sentence proved the truth. Since then, he had remained close to her family by moving to San Antonio. He needed to be near those who loved Hillary as much as he did. He didn't see them as often as he should, and it wasn't because of how they felt, but mostly because of how he felt. Moving to San Antonio was a penance he'd willingly paid. He felt that he needed to punish himself. He would have to spend the rest of his life in the city his wife had been brutally murdered. Was he a masochist? Absolutely. But he owed it to his wife and child to never forget. His own parents worried that he was past the point of no return. They feared they'd lost him forever when he lost Hillary and the baby. In some ways it was the truth. The man who left home and joined the Army was gone. The Army had made him a better man and husband. That was until Hillary was murdered. Then the very worst of him took over. If Ethan and Steve hadn't met him at the prison gates, he wasn't sure what he would've done.

Three months before his release, Bench had an unexpected visitor. Two, actually. Steve and Ethan had flown in to offer him a job that he'd neither inquired about nor immediately accepted. He sat there listening to the two veterans speak of their company and all the good they did.

"What do you say, Bench?"

It felt right being called by his moniker. For the past three years he'd been simply called Phelan. He was no longer Sergeant First Class, just as he was no longer Bench to his Delta brothers.

"How did you get in to see me?" Bench asked ignoring their question.

"We are on the list of approved visitors," Ethan answered, not showing his hand.

"No, you aren't. Besides, only people I have a prior relationship with are allowed on the list. So again, how did you get in to see me?"

Bench had spent the past three years learning everything he could about military law, not that he was going to appeal his sentence. He deserved the time spent. He'd instructed his Delta team to stop loading his commissary funds, not that they listened. His team had his six, which was something he'd never forget, but how these two men were standing before him, he didn't understand.

"This is true. Your name was supplied to us by someone within the intelligence community. We aren't privy to the records from your court-martial, but we were able to talk with your team. If we were in your situation, I suspect we would've acted the same way. Now, let me tell you about the ECP Bravo team. I think you may be interested in the new manhunter's team we're building," Ethan said as he motioned for Bench to return to the seat he'd yet to occupy.

Now years later, and neither Ethan nor Steve had explained who gave them the tip, but whoever this person was, he'd saved Bench's life.

* * *

With their last mission behind them, Bench and Doc were meeting at the gym to get some boxing in. For the past six months, he'd worked side by side with Doc to build her physical strength up, but his primary goal was to help ease some of her anxiety after her kidnapping. He still remembered that day... How could he not? The team had walked in while she was being raped. As much as he'd wanted to make the Nigerian crime lord suffer, it was more imperative to get Susan away quickly. That had been the first time he'd let his anger resurface on a mission.

"Hey," Susan said as she gave him a side hug. This also was an improvement. For months, not only had she stopped talking, but no one with the exception of Liam could touch her. Little by little, she was returning into the spitfire she'd once been.

"You ready to get pummeled today?"

"As if," she shot back, then got serious. "Bench, I know you've been holding back, but I want you to really teach me. I can take it."

No way could she take the beast he kept locked away. That animal only came out when he was in an MMA fight, and even then he attempted to pull back so he wouldn't kill anyone. However, the closer he got to *that* day, the less restraint he had.

"Sure thing, Tiny."

"Hey!" she replied as she punched him in his bicep.

"I think it's time to throw in some more martial arts. Get padded up and I'll meet you in the ring."

This was what Bench needed. A light sparring with Doc and then a real match afterwards.

Years earlier, Bench had accepted this was his new life. It was time to suck it up, as Bama always said.

CHAPTER 3

Avery tried not to get all girly with her new job, but hello! It was more money than she'd ever made writing. Heck, it was more money than she'd made collectively in three years.

Pulling out her notebook, she began jotting down what she needed to do and in what order.

1) Take the advance and apply it to this month's rent. Knowing she had a place to live would clear her mind and keep her focused on the job.

2) Buy writing supplies. She'd need index cards and push pins. She had already cleared off her existing notes for a book topic she'd considered writing. She'd almost resorted to writing romance novels instead of true crime or nonfiction. At some point she just needed to make some money. She'd also looked into self-publishing, and hadn't rejected that idea. Many authors had been successful by stepping away from large publishing houses. The self-publishing market opened up other options, much like paid tv subscriptions had done to cable and satellite companies. The days of cable or antennas were long gone, and it was time for the cable

companies to realize they no longer had the upper hand. Free commerce was a beautiful thing.

She also needed to pick up some essential supplies; Twizzlers and cherry cola. She would need the sugar since she had a tendency to lose track of time and forget to eat.

3) Research all the victim files, make contact with their family members.

4) Speak with law enforcement. She knew this would be just as difficult as getting interviews with the victim's families. Not everyone would want to relive the worst moments in their lives. However, that wasn't the case with everyone. A few had made the circuit of talk shows, news stations, and radio interviews. They needed to let out their anger and frustration. They were hoping for a champion. These were the ones she'd talk with first. She figured she'd get a pretty good gauge of their interest based on the number of news articles and interviews they've done in the past.

5) Arrange for a face to face meeting with Ramsey. Thinking of him as Jared made him feel too real. She'd maintain distance by using his last name, or so she hoped. She decided to not meet with him until she'd researched everything she could with the victims and interviewed their families. Callum had given her two weeks, so she wanted a full understanding of what he did to each victim, and if the killings varied in any way.

6) Look at the copycat killer. What similarities were there, if any? Were the same police officers working this case? Did the families have any insight or thoughts on why the killer picked Ramsey to copy?

She realized she had more questions than answers at this point. After she finished with the first task, she moved to the second one shopping for supplies. It was a dangerous thing for writers or creative people in general to stop at any supply stores. Each year she stocked up on binders, paper, folders, and sticky notepads during the back-to-school sales. When else could she find colored pencils for a dollar, or reams of notebook paper for fifty cents? Opening her supply closet, which was the closet in the spare room, aka her office, she picked through her stash and found the highlighters and pens she preferred. Avery was a pen and paper girl. Before she turned on her computer, she would outline her objectives, speculations, and theories on paper. Eventually, she'd transfer everything over to a Word file, but nothing felt more productive than being able to highlight completed tasks.

She'd also decided to keep track of her hours. This wasn't necessary for her pay, but she was an analytical person and had a double major in marketing. She knew how important it was to know if there was an ROI, return on her investment. If she was making ten grand for two weeks, she wanted to know what her hourly rate would come out to. She had a friend who had spent over three thousand hours writing in one year, grossed ten grand, netted six. She was excited about her earnings, until she did an hourly rate analysis. She'd made three bucks an hour. Once she took out her expenses, she was at two dollars an hour. Realizing she couldn't live on that income, she'd turned her writing into part time and became a bank teller during the day. This was what Avery needed to know, at least so she could tell her parents how successful she'd been. Oh, who was she kidding? They wouldn't count this assignment as a win. It would be a temporary bonus, and not something she'd be able to make a living at, or at least that's what her parents would say.

'Get out of your head. Geez, you're thirty-five years old. Stop acting like a ten-year-old.'

Now that her peptalk was done, she continued to make notes of her questions before turning on her laptop three hours later.

Pushing up her sweater sleeve, and yes, she had on a sweater in Texas. Her office didn't have windows. As such, there wasn't any sunlight streaming in to warm her. The room was ridiculously small, so no matter where she put her desk, the air vent hit her directly. But she wasn't complaining. Her two-story, two-bedroom loft townhouse was just right for her and her crazy beagle, Bailey, who was always excited to see Avery come home. Bailey was her constant companion while she was writing, generally sleeping under her desk.

"Come on, Bailey Girl. Let's get your walk in before it gets too late. Mommy has a lot of work to do."

* * *

It was time to get busy. First the families of the victims. She'd already pinned index cards on her bulletin board of the victims, known facts, like age, sex, race, occupation, and the location their bodies were found. The second card had details of their families. Stepping back and reviewing her storyboard, she began to let her mind create assumptions. This was something the law enforcement agencies shied away from. They worked on facts. But a writer drew a story from speculation, and would see how the facts supported it.

The victims ranged in age and sex. They were different nationalities and local residents, with the exception of his last victim. Hillary Phelan was not only eight months pregnant, but she was also in San Antonio for a baby shower from her family. This had to be a crime of opportunity, didn't it? Were the others? Were they targeted or randomly chosen? Until Hillary, she'd assumed they were targeted. They were all locals. His first victim was a convenience store owner. He'd been killed after he'd closed up the store for the night. Most stores were open 24/7, but Mr. Hamish closed early that day. Why? What caused the police to retroactively identify him as victim one? She'd always heard the first kill was crucial in the killer's spree. So why a fifty-five-year-old community supporter and business owner? Had Mr. Hamish had an argument with Ramsey previously? Was he targeted because of his race and nationality? What was Ramsey's link to the victim, if any?

Avery wrote her questions under his picture. And followed the same process with the remaining victims, ending with Hillary and her child. This was the one that stumped her. They all had at some point, but this one was unique... She was pregnant. None of his other victims were, at least she didn't think so. One more thing to do... pull death certificates. Did the killer ramp up his sickness by taking out two at the same time? How did she cross his path? And most importantly, why did the police link her to the RWS, as she called the River Walk Strangler, especially since Hillary wasn't found near the River Walk?

What commonality did these eight victims have for the police to link them together? Did he leave a calling card? Did he take souvenirs? Was there something physically linking them? She didn't know, but she wouldn't stop digging. Eventually she'd have more answers than questions, but until then she had a lot of work to do.

Placing her index finger at the edge of her lip, she began her research with his first victim.

"Tell me all about yourself, Hamish. Why did Ramsey kill you?"

CHAPTER 4

Trying to twist out the kinks in her neck, Avery reviewed her notes from her most recent interview. Carley Wright had been victim number six. Just like the previous five, it appeared she was randomly chosen, but something didn't feel right. She couldn't put her finger on it, but there was something she had missed. She wondered if the police had missed it too. She had an appointment with Texas Ranger Dax Chambers that afternoon. He had been the lead on Ramsey's case. She wanted to know how they caught him. Was it by accident like the Son of Sam and his unpaid parking tickets? Had it been a tip like Jeffrey Dahmer? Or was he too arrogant and caught by flaunting his kills to the police like the BTK killer? Did he have a job that led him to his kills? There had to be a link. Most killers hid in plain sight and appeared to be normal, intelligent men in the community.

Because of her research, she knew these serial killers were only a drop in the bucket of the deranged murderers still not arrested. Chills ran down her arms at the thought.

She knew this project would be scary, but to know that most serial killers were only caught by sheer luck was terrifying.

Avery gathered her notes and stuffed them into her laptop case. She knew law enforcement wouldn't disclose any more than they had to, and she'd eventually have to go visit Jared Ramsey herself. That was one task she wasn't eager to do, but she had a job to do, and she was a professional.

'Get a grip! You knew this would be challenging.'

* * *

Avery tucked the loose hair behind her ear. She'd dressed conservatively and tied her shoulder-length brunette hair in a knot at the base of her neck. Her mother had always stressed the need to dress for the job you want, not the one you have. As much as she regularly ignored her mother's opinion, this was one she believed in. When the tall Ranger stepped into the lobby, she tried not to let his Stetson hat and rugged good looks intimidate her, but she was a woman, and he definitely cut a powerful and authoritative appearance.

Swallowing her girly instincts to fawn, she offered him her hand instead.

"Ranger Chambers, thank you for agreeing to meet with me."

The expression on the Ranger's face didn't mask his frustration. She knew he wasn't interested in being part of the interview, but he also knew the value of the press, even if she wasn't a reporter.

"No problem. Follow me." It wasn't a request or suggestion; it was an order. He was letting her know he wasn't going to coddle her, not that she expected it.

When the two entered the conference room, she was

surprised to see the FBI agent who had worked on capturing Ramsey.

"Agent Cruz," she stated, once again extending her hand. The agent seemed more relaxed with her presence.

"Miss Grey," he acknowledged before offering her a seat around the circular table.

"I wasn't expecting to see you, but I appreciate your time, both of yours."

"What do you want to know?" Dax asked, again not hiding his frustration.

"As I mentioned on the phone, I'm doing research for Callum Easton." She was contractually forbidden from disclosing that she was his ghostwriter, and instead used researcher as her job title.

When neither man reacted to her statement, she continued.

"Mr. Easton's next book focuses on serial killers. However, unlike the numerous books on the topic, he's looking for a more localized investigation, which is why I'm here. Jared Ramsey was the first serial killer caught in San Antonio. Now that he has a copycat killer, it would be helpful to understand as much as I can about Mr. Ramsey's motivations."

"His motivations? If you know anything about serial killers, you'd know a motive isn't exactly necessary. They are driven by depravity, ego, and the desire to kill as many people as they can," Dax spat out. He hated talking with reporters, and this one was just like any other. He would've rejected the request, but Callum Easton had more pull than most writers, and Avery's brother was a fellow Ranger.

"As my colleague said, there's never one single reason for someone to kill," Agent Cruz stated. "Ramsey was no different. He craved notoriety and fame."

"Did he taunt law enforcement like others had?"

"Each kill was a taunt," Dax answered.

"But to answer your question, he didn't send notes to us, nor did he leave us any clues," Cruz answered.

"But obviously there was something that prompted you to believe the murders were all done by the same person. Would you share what that was?"

She didn't miss the look between the two. She doubted they would answer her question, so when the Ranger replied she was shocked.

"We never revealed what that was, however you could find out by looking at his trial transcripts. Ramsey kept souvenirs from the victims. Each souvenir was unique to each victim."

"Such as?"

"The third victim was recently engaged. Ramsey cut her ring finger off but left the ring," Cruz answered.

"The fifth victim was going bald and had spoken to a plastic surgeon about transplants. Ramsey had colored the man's scalp with a black marker and left a Chia plant at the scene."

"So they were targeted. He had to have followed them to know such things," Avery thought out loud.

"Yes. The only one that didn't fit the stalking theory was the last victim. She wasn't a local, she'd only arrived that morning for a baby shower. He wouldn't have been able to follow her. She'd driven straight to her sister's house."

"The only time she'd left was an hour before her murder," Cruz added.

"And you're sure it was Ramsey?"

"Positive."

"Can I ask why you believe so?"

The men shared another look, but eventually Dax answered.

"Again, all of this is in the trial transcripts. I suggest you get a copy of the report. Mrs. Phelan was here for a baby shower, her own. Her son was removed post-mortem and left on her chest, sans the umbilical cord."

"Oh my God," Avery said as she covered her mouth in horror.

"Out of the eight murders, hers was the most gruesome, and the most puzzling. His killings were all disturbing but not nearly as much as Mrs. Phelan's. She didn't fit any of the profiles we'd made."

Agent Cruz continued the recounting, "We first wondered if Ramsey had any ties to her husband, but we never could link them. His random kill still remains a mystery."

"I don't understand. Did he not confess to her death?"

"He did," Dax said. "However, he never gave us a reason for the change in pattern."

"And the copycat? Does he follow the same pattern?"

Cruz shook his head, "Sorry Ms. Grey, that's an active case. We can't and won't talk about any similarities."

'So there are similarities,' she surmised. She wasn't sure if it was the similar to victims one to seven or as random and depraved as his eighth and ninth murders. Wondering about the last victim, she asked whether they counted the infant as victim number nine.

"At the trial there was a lot of debate over this, but as far as law enforcement is concerned, the infant was his ninth victim. He was developed far enough that he could've survived outside of his mother's womb."

"That's horrible. Her poor husband."

Again, the two men shared a look that made her wonder what she was missing. She'd left Joe Phelan several messages, but he'd not returned a single one. She knew this was to be expected by distraught family members, but the other seven had eventually agreed to an interview. What did these officers know that they weren't sharing?

"I've tried to reach out to him, but he hasn't returned any of my calls."

Dax nodded in understanding. They knew he would never agree to an interview. In speaking with his former coworker Jack Hunter, Dax knew Joe kept all the events close to his chest. He wasn't even sure Joe's coworkers knew about the murders.

"He's unlikely to agree," Cruz responded. "To my knowledge, he's never spoken to anyone outside of his immediate family and law enforcement."

"He confuses me. Most people move away from the city or town where something like this happens, but not him. He moved here, to the scene of the crime. Don't you find that strange? Plus, he wasn't at the trial, at least not that I've seen. Why come here and not go to the trial?"

Neither man responded, so she continued. "I've thought about calling his co-workers. He works at a security protection company, but I'm not sure if they could provide me with any useful information."

"I doubt they even know. He's not someone to give unnecessary or useful information," Cruz stated.

"Not useful? His wife and child were murdered, by a serial killer no less. How is that not necessary information, especially at a protection company? What if he had a setback? What if he couldn't protect someone because of a flashback? Isn't that something his employers would be afraid of happening?"

"I'm familiar with ECP, we both are. They are professionals to the highest degree. I have no doubt the owners are aware of his circumstances and wouldn't take any unnecessary risks, to both their clients or Bench himself," Cruz replied.

"Bench?"

"Oh, sorry. That's his call name from the Army. He goes by it at ECP as well."

"Um, that's helpful. Do you think it'd be useful to contact his former Commanding Officer?"

Again with the looks...

"I wouldn't recommend it. Besides, the military's not going to talk about his situation. If you want to know more about Bench, you'll have to talk with him yourself... If he lets you. I'd be careful poking around in his life."

"Is he dangerous?" She hadn't worried about her safety when interviewing the other victim's families, so why would she be cautious around Mr. Phelan?

"Not to you. He's just not someone I'd push."

"So don't poke the bear?" she asked the FBI agent.

For the first time, the men grinned before agreeing with her analogy.

"Well, I want to thank you for your help. I understand the copycat killer is still an active investigation, but I'm going to keep digging. I'm hoping to find something that will help me understand his motives."

"Ms. Grey, be careful. This killer is more sporadic than his predecessor. These are not men you should taunt."

"Men? Do you think there's a team of two this time?"

"No, Ms. Grey. I'm saying that you need to back away from Ramsey, and the killer. For that matter, I'd stay away from Bench as well," Cruz advised.

"Is there any chance they are one in the same?" She'd wondered that before. It wouldn't be the first time a victim's family member lost their moral compass. Plus, he was ex-military. He was more than capable to carry out murders.

"Not a single one," Dax spat. "Don't go looking for trouble. That's what we're saying. The last thing you want is to be in the killer's scope. Watch your back, Ms. Grey. Killers change patterns all the time, just like Ramsey did. Don't put yourself in the killer's path. This is not a game of chicken. You will lose."

"Got it. Well, gentlemen, thank you for your time. I hope you find this killer."

"We will," Cruz reassured.

Avery said her goodbyes and once again decided to reach out to the elusive Bench.

"Mr. Phelan, this is Avery Grey again. I've just left a meeting with Texas Ranger Chambers and Special Agent Cruz of the FBI. I have some follow-up questions. Please contact me at..."

CHAPTER 5

"When is she going to give up?" Bench asked as he deleted the voicemail once again. Had Dax and Cruz sent her to him? He knew he hadn't been the most cooperative when they were looking for Ramsey, but to send a reporter his way didn't make sense.

He'd done some research on Avery Grey after her first call. Not that there was a lot to find. She was thirty-five and a San Antonio local. She had a journalism degree from A&M. She had been engaged to ENT, Dr. Jeffery Sanders, but called off the wedding. Her brother was a Texas Ranger, and she was a struggling writer. Now she was working with NY bestseller Callum Easton. He was a household name, and not just in San Antonio. Several of his books were used in trial cases, and he had served as an expert witness for a couple of recent murders. He was the real deal, not that it mattered to Bench. He wouldn't be talking with either of them.

Hearing Avery's call reminded him to contact the prison in Huntsville. He needed to remind them of his upcoming visit. Even though he'd never missed his monthly visit, he always called to alert them of his arrival. Some would say he was a masochist, but he didn't think so. He wanted to make sure Jared Ramsey never forgot his face. As for him, Bench needed to look the devil in the eyes.

Tossing his gym clothes in his bag, he headed out of the apartment twenty minutes later. It was time to forget about Jared Ramsey and the pesky journalist, Avery Grey. It was time for him to face his next opponent. Pain made his days and nights more tolerable.

Before he walked into the gym his cell phone rang. He ignored the call, assuming it was the writer once more. When it rang again, he pulled it out of his back pocket, planning on declining the call. Only it wasn't Avery. Ethan was calling him directly. Most mission updates came from Turbo or Dodger, their team leader. Accepting the call, he listened as he was given strict orders to return to the office.

"We have a job?"

"No, we have a problem. Now get in," Ethan replied.

This couldn't be good. He'd rarely heard such tight restraint in his boss's voice.

"On my way," Bench replied as he tossed his bag into the backseat.

'What now?'

When Bench walked into the ECP offices, he was met at the door by Ethan and Steve. He followed them into the conference room, where he came face to face with Ranger Chambers and Special Agent Cruz. He knew immediately this had something to do with the writer.

"We had a visit today from Avery Grey. Do you know who that is?" Cruz asked the group.

Bench nodded. "She's the writer who's been interviewing the families of Ramsey's victims."

"She's working with Callum Easton on Ramsey's killing spree primarily. However, she's also digging into the copycat killer," Dax said.

"I'm not going to be interviewed by her. She can call anyone she wants... it's not happening."

"And that's what we told her. However, she's determined to hear from you so much that she mentioned tracking you down through ECP or the Army. She isn't going to be easy to push aside," Cruz stated.

"Are you telling me to grant the interview?" Bench barked. He wasn't going to be pressured by some twit looking for a bestseller.

"No, not that we even could. We just wanted you to know that she's going around you to get the interview. If she reaches out to ECP, your coworkers or your Army buddies, Hillary's death will be known by all. As far as we know, you've kept the details pretty private."

"As private as I can for a high-profile murder case," Bench grunted. "This copycat killer is putting more focus on Ramsey's murders. I've received calls from several reporters asking for my thoughts."

"You've not said anything," Ethan stated without reprimand or reproof.

"Why would I? I've not told anyone here about Hillary. It was only a few months ago that it was discovered I was married. Unless you had Turbo or Blaze dig into my background."

"That wouldn't happen," Steve reassured.

"How did you two know?" Bench asked Steve and Ethan.

"Although we knew enough before we hired you, it wasn't relevant to your position nor was it our place to divulge it," Ethan stated.

"Thank you for respecting my privacy. If only the media would. So what do you suggest I do with this woman? Aside from giving her an interview."

"We're not here to advise you on how to handle Ms. Grey. We just wanted you to know she's digging, and most likely will continue to do so, until she gets information about your wife and son."

"How much does she know?" Steve asked.

"As much as the trial records. She knows Hillary was victim eight and nine. So also knows Ramsey was not caught by our leads," Dax stated.

"She played ignorant about the specifics, but she knew more than she let on. She's a researcher. We discovered she already had the trial transcripts before coming to see us... which she played dumb about. But her questions reaffirmed what we suspected. She's good, really good," Cruz said.

"I don't care how good she is. I'm not going to speak with her. She can do whatever she wants. If anyone is interested in my life, let them dig. I have no secrets, not anymore."

Bench stood from the table and nodded to the four men, two from his past and two in his present life. His past and future were colliding all because of some nosy woman.

Instead of leaving the office, he stopped by his desk and pulled up the search folder he had for Avery Grey. A few clicks later he had the information he needed. Armed with her picture, address, and email address, he left the office knowing what his next step would be.

* * *

To: Avery Grey

From: Joe Phelan

Re: Let it go!

Ms. Grey, I have received all seven of your voicemails. If you can't tell already, let me make it clear... I'm not going to do an interview with you or anyone else. I have no desire to bring up past pain and suffering. I have spoken with law enforcement and know you're determined to seek answers to your intrusive questions, even if it means reaching out to my friends and coworkers. I am asking you to respect my privacy and that of my family. If you attempt to contact my employer or anyone from my former Army team, I assure you I will contact the authorities about your continued harassment.

I will have a harassment restraining order issued against you and Callum Easton. According to Texas state laws, harassment takes on many forms, including verbal and emotional abuse, if the abuser (you) intentionally causes emotional harm to a victim (me). Let this email serve as notice to cease and desist from your continuous attempts to contact me.

Joe Phelan

CHAPTER 6

Avery read the email for a second time. A cease and desist order? Was she really harassing him if he chose to not acknowledge her calls? Did she want to find out? That was a no-way Jose.

'And to threaten Callum, wow he has a lot of nerve.'

She closed the email browser and went into the kitchen. This called for a glass of wine, a stout vintage. After she opened and poured herself a glass of Argentinian Malbec, she called her best friend, Janie.

"What are you drinking?" Janie said once the call was connected.

"Wine. Why? And hello to you too."

"What kind of wine?"

"Um... Janie, what's up with the questions?"

"What kind of wine are you drinking?"

"A malbec. Why?"

"What's wrong?"

"Janie, this is the strangest conversation we've ever had, and that's saying something. Why did you ask about my wine?"

"When you have wine, I can tell if you're celebrating or stressing by the varietal. Malbec definitely puts you in the stressing category. So what's wrong?"

Avery loved her former college roommate and reigning bestie. She'd never correlated her drinking choices with her temperament, but Janie was correct. She was stressed. It wasn't just the email and harassment threats... it was what she discovered from the FBI and Ranger. The depravity of Ramsey went further than she'd realized. She'd pulled the court transcripts, but hadn't reviewed them all. There were thousands of pages to read, and now she had no choice but to read each and every word.

"I had a hard day. Well, for one thing I met with law enforcement about the River Walk Strangler. He was one sick man."

"Of course he was. What did you expect?"

"I don't know. It was just hearing about it, especially since I'm going to see him tomorrow, has put me on edge."

"Did you just say you were going to the prison to meet with a serial killer?"

"Yes, of course I am. I have a job to do."

Janie was the only person she'd confided in, and that was before she signed the confidentiality agreement. Even though she wasn't supposed to talk about the book, Janie knew the basics, and Avery needed someone to bounce things off of.

"Your job sucks then. Now, what's the second thing?"

"How did you know?"

"You said the meeting with the police was one thing... so there's more."

"I think I might need some legal advice. Can I send you a dollar through PayPal as a retainer?"

"I think I still owe you ten dollars from last weekend, so we'll call it even. Why do you think you need my services?"

Avery read the email to Janie and waited in silence for her friend, now legal advisor, to jump in.

When she didn't do so quickly, Avery prompted her. "Well, does he have a case?"

"I'd have to look at how the law is written. I understood it to be used in domestic abuse cases. As a member of the press, you'd have more license under the first amendment."

"But I'm not a reporter. I'm a researcher."

"But you are a journalist. The first amendment should protect you. However, you can't ever be one hundred percent sure you're not at risk for a defamation lawsuit. Since you can write about the murder, you'd have to be careful how you disclose anything about the victims or their families. Since he'd made it abundantly clear he would take legal actions, I'd err on the side of caution and leave him alone."

"I feel like there's a story there. I mean, I realize it's never easy to remember things like this, but the others that I've interviewed were concerned about the copycat killer, but that's not so with Joe. He's a roadblock, which you know makes him even more interesting to me. What's he hiding?"

"Probably nothing. Avery, remember he lost two people that day. I suggest you move on and leave Joe Phelan to his own demons and concentrate on getting the best manuscript you can for Callum."

"You're right. I just hate being shut down. My first reaction is to double down, but I'll let it go. Should I respond to his email?"

"No. Just wipe your hands of him and his opinions. Now, let's get back to you going to Huntsville tomorrow. Why? Avery, it doesn't matter if he's behind bars, he's evil incarnate."

"I have to go. This is the first time he's agreed to an interview. The warden has granted me an hour to interview

Ramsey. I've already written up my questions and submitted them to the Warden."

"Why does he need them?"

"He has to make sure I'm genuinely going to conduct an interview. I don't have the credentials that they'd expect. Apparently, there are people who pretend to be writers so they can get close to a prisoner, especially serial killers. Can you imagine someone falling victim to a killer's charm? It baffles me."

"There's a lot of gullible and misguided people out there. Just be careful. Have a guard stay with you. Don't take any unnecessary risks. Promise me."

"I promise. Honestly, I'm not sure what to expect. I've watched enough TV to know there are several different ways to meet with a prisoner. Using a phone, face to face with a guard in the room, or in a general area with other prisoners meeting their families."

"He's a freaking serial killer, Avery! I doubt they will have him in a casual setting. I personally hope you interview him through plexiglass and a phone. I really wish you wouldn't go at all."

"I'll be okay. Now tell me about your day. What are you drinking?"

"I was drinking soda until you told me about tomorrow. Now I'm chugging Riesling."

The two giggled and Avery half-heartedly listened as her friend talked about her new case. She'd only half listened because the other half of her attention was spent thinking about Joe "Bench" Phelan.

'What are you hiding, Bench?'

* * *

Avery drove into the parking lot of the Texas State Penitentiary in Huntsville and was directed to the unit where maximum-security prisoners were kept. She jumped when the first bars closed behind her with a loud clang. Avery followed the guard into a room with three solid concrete walls and one with a large mirror. She felt reassured knowing that someone might possibly be on the other side of the wall, looking out for her… Even if it was a false sense of security.

"Wait here. The prisoner already has a visitor." Looking at his watch, he then informed her it would only be a five-minute wait.

Avery had thought the interview would take place in the room she was sitting in, so she took the time to pull out her manilla folder and once again review her notes, not that she needed to. She knew the questions by heart. But when the guard opened the door, she once again jumped.

"Follow me, Miss Grey."

The guard was walking fast, so Avery had to nearly jog to keep up with him. That was when she ran smack into a hard body. Large strong arms steadied her and when she finally looked up, she gasped.

"Mr. Phelan?" She wasn't questioning if it was him, but more like why he was there.

"Miss Grey," he said as he nodded to the guard, and stepped away from Avery. Even though she'd seen his picture in her files, she was still shocked by his presence, and even more so that he recognized her.

It wasn't until the security guard spoke, that she realized they were still standing side by side.

"See you next month," the guard said, and then led Avery past Bench toward the next closed door.

Avery couldn't help but watch the behemoth of a man stiffen, and clench and unclench his fist, as he nodded to the guard and walked in the other direction, with another guard by his side.

"Do you know Joe?" The guard by her side asked.

"Not really. I guess I'm just surprised to see him visiting Ramsey."

"To tell the truth, Joe comes once a month, and on the anniversary of his wife's death."

"Every month? That's strange."

"No, what's strange is that he never speaks to Ramsey. He just silently sits across from him staring down at his wife's murderer."

"He never speaks?"

"Not a word. He sits with his arms folded and glares at Ramsey. If you ask me, he's never going to get over his wife's death as long as he continues to visit each month."

Avery let the guard's words sink in.

'Why come to see Ramsey and not demand answers? There are so many layers within Joe Phelan.'

CHAPTER 7

Bench hadn't meant to growl at the writer, but he hadn't been expecting to see her, and definitely not at the prison. Not that he should've been surprised. She'd already proven she was tenacious and determined to get her story. But to meet with a convicted serial killer was a risk she shouldn't have to take. Had he been the reason she'd shown up at the prison?

Since he was released from Leavenworth, Bench had made his monthly visit with Hillary's murder. He never spoke to Ramsey. He simply sat across from the man who had single-handedly ruined his life and his future. The satisfaction he'd first seen when he visited Ramsey had eventually turned into boredom. Ramsey had initially taunted Bench. Giving him graphic details of his wife and son's murder. Bench never showed any signs of distress. However, once he exited the prison, he'd lost his hold on his stomach contents. Bench wanted to hit someone, which was how he found himself in the MMA gymnasium. The need to feel pain and let his demons out was overwhelming. Nodding to the gym owner, he walked into the locker room and began changing into his athletic shorts and tee shirt.

The owner met him outside the room, tossing Bench a roll of tape. Even though he wouldn't be fighting an opponent that evening, he needed hand wraps to protect his wrists and knuckles. Over the next four hours, Bench worked his core. All the areas under stress in a fight were vulnerable and needed strengthening. From deadlifts to squats, Bench relished the muscle strains.

While in the military he hadn't had his current physique. As a Delta, he needed to be able to deadlift the average weight of a person. His core, legs, back, shoulders and chest were always being strengthened. However, while in prison, he used the time to bulk up. He exceeded his moniker Bench, by bench pressing over three hundred pounds in a deadlift.

"Hey, Phelan," one of the organizers called out.

Bench held the boxing bag still while he waited for Rudy to get to him.

"What's up, Rudy?"

"Nothing good, that's for sure." Bench didn't question that statement. He knew firsthand how underhanded Rudy could be, especially if there was money on the table.

"Did you need something?"

"Oh yeah, sorry. I know you're working out, but I wanted to know if you'd be interested in a match tonight. My man has the flu and can't make it. I'd rather not cancel the fight, so what do you say, big man? You up to a match?"

Bench didn't typically book matches without his promoter, but he did have a lot of frustration to work off. Not only was Avery Grey blowing up his phone and threatening to call his friends, but now she's meeting with that psychopath. Then there was the date. Five years ago, he'd been celebrating a different anniversary. Now he lived with a constant reminder of what he'd lost. So was he ready to throw some punches? Yes, but he also knew not to trust Rudy.

"Have you spoken with Ricardo? He's not a fan of yours, but he is my promoter."

"You know Ricky and I have a difference of opinion sometimes," Rudy stated, then chuckled when he heard Bench snort back a response.

"Fine, I haven't talked to him. I didn't know who I was going to get as a replacement. You just happen to be here. So what do you say?"

"Who's the opponent?" Bench didn't want to hurt a newbie, and he knew that in his current mood he wouldn't hold back from his punches.

"Razor. You guys have fought before."

"If you call it a fight. I walked away just fine. Are you sure he wants a rematch?"

"Oh, I'm sure. He hasn't talked about anything else for months. You in?"

"Yeah, I'm in. I'll let Ricardo know."

After Bench was given the details, he placed a call to Ricardo Sanchez. They met right after he joined the gym. Unlike other promoters, Ricardo wasn't involved because of the money. He understood the need to eradicate demons through blows. That's not to say that he hadn't profited from working with Bench. Bench, however, never kept his winnings. He gave them to various gym owners to support boys or girls who needed an escape but couldn't afford the monthly dues.

"I'm not sure Razor will play nice tonight, but I also know what today is. You're more tense on the twelfth of each month. I've never asked you why, but I've linked them together. Someday you'll trust me enough to tell me why the twelfth is so bad."

"Not likely. And you're right, Razor is looking for

payback. I'm sure it will be a no holds barred battle. So, are you coming down?"

"You know I am. I'll make some arrangements for my kids. My wife is on duty tonight, and it was my night to watch them, but I'm sure my sister would love to have them overnight."

"You're sure?"

"I won't leave you alone with Razor or Rudy. Neither will have your back. See you in an hour."

Bench went to the showers and wondered if anyone else had associated his bad days with the twelfth of each month.

CHAPTER 8

Avery watched as Jared Ramsey scuffled into the room. His orange jumpsuit hung loosely over his medium size frame. She couldn't see his smile because of his ratty beard, but she knew it was there. His eyes appeared to be reflecting his mood.

He didn't wait until he was seated to address her.

"You're so much better to look at than my last visitor."

"Mr. Phelan. I hear he comes every month. Do you have other visitors?"

"Avery, I don't want to talk about that shell of a man. I want to talk about you."

"And I want to talk about you."

"Very well, I think a bargain should be discussed. I'll answer every question you ask for every one of mine you answer."

"That's not how an interview works."

"It is for me. Take it or leave it."

Avery watched how relaxed he was, and knew this interview was more important to her than him. She also knew he wasn't playing chicken. He'd have no problem walking out of the room.

"Two for one. I get to ask you two questions for every one you ask, and you have to tell the truth."

Jared smirked. He hadn't expected her to renegotiate the terms, but he liked it and nodded his approval.

"Great, I'll go first," Avery stated.

"Sorry, no can do. You might decide to leave after your first two questions." Jared kept his eyes focused on her, while running his fingers through his beard, as if weighing his first question.

"Avery. I'm assuming I can call you that."

"Is that a question?" Avery smirked. He had no idea who he was playing with. She'd spent most of her childhood trying to best and circumvent her brother's taunting. She might not be evil like Ramsey, but she wasn't a pushover either.

"Fair enough, let's drop the formalities. I'll call you Avery, and you can call me Jared."

Avery nodded and waited for his first question.

"Are you married?"

"No. Now it's my turn. Would you have stopped killing if you hadn't been captured?"

"No." He didn't hide the gleam in his eyes. He enjoyed the hunt and eventually the endorphins released when he took a life.

"Did you stalk your victims?"

"Victims?" He scoffed.

"Did you stalk them? All of them?" She asked again.

"Yes and no. All but the last two."

"Hillary and her child were the two. Is that who you're referring to?"

"Nope, you had your two questions. Now, it's my turn." He waited for her to object, but when she didn't, he continued. "Are you in a relationship? Remember, we have to be honest."

"The only person in my bed is my dog. Now back to my original question. Are you referring to Hillary Phelan and her baby as your last two victims that you didn't stalk?"

"Yes. I didn't realize she was pregnant when I selected her."

"If you had known, would it have stopped you from killing her?"

"No, it was a bonus. Two for one, just like our interview." Once again Jared smirked. He knew throwing her own words back to Avery was malicious, but he was enjoying himself too much.

"Now tell me about your dog."

"My dog?"

"Yes, my question is about your dog."

Avery knew he was trying to lower her defenses with his softball question, but she'd play his game, at least for now.

"She's a beagle, and her name is Bailey."

Jared nodded as if he approved of her expanding her answer. She was hoping he'd do the same.

"How did you pick the other seven victims?"

"Again with the *victims*."

Avery wrote something on her notepad while Jared continued with his answer.

"It wasn't hard to find them. They weren't victims."

Avery's impulse was to ask why, but she'd save that for later. She wasn't sure how long he'd continue playing their game.

"Very well. What did they have in common then?"

"Who said they had commonalities?"

"You did. If you believe they weren't victims, then you believed they deserved to die. I want to know why. And remember, you have to tell the truth."

"But Avery, I can tell you the truth without giving you an explanation."

"True, but I believe you want to explain yourself. You want people to know why you were delivering justice."

Jared thought about what she'd said and agreed. "They were all abusers."

"How so?"

"That's two questions already."

"Nope, you ignored the first one." Jared was about to object, when she then reminded him of her initial question, and him claiming they weren't victims.

"So I answered it."

"No, you didn't. Now, how were they abusers?"

"Have you dug through their backgrounds yet?"

"Apparently not thoroughly enough."

"Fine. I'll let you figure out who did what, but here's the list of sins. Wife beater, drug dealer, power abuser, a cheater, and a thief."

"That's only five What about the others?"

"I shouldn't answer that, but I'm enjoying this so much. Who's to say that only one was a drug dealer?"

"Were they?"

"Sorry, it's my turn. Why are you a researcher and not the author of this book?"

"It's not easy to get into the publishing world. You do what you have to do to put food on the table."

"Or food in Bailey's bowl."

"Yes. Let's say I believe you were on a vigilante mission, ridding the abusers from society. Why take Hillary's life, and that of her poor baby?"

Jared couldn't hold back his lecherous grin. Avery immediately understood that killing Hillary and her child had changed his targets. He enjoyed killing her and the baby. Avery could feel the bile rising, urgently trying to expel itself. She wanted answers, but she was dreading what came next.

"I think you already know why. It's written all over your face. Are you going to be sick if I tell you how watching the light drain out of her beautiful eyes gave me a thirst for more blood? Or that taking that child from its protective womb caused an erection? Does going into details make you see me as a monster?"

"I already see you as a monster. I think that's why you killed her. You wanted to know how it felt to kill a random, innocent person. I believe your MO would have changed if you hadn't been caught."

"That's a lot of assumptions."

"But they're true, aren't they?"

"Is that your second question?"

"No. My question is about the copycat killer. Do you know who it is?"

"Yes."

"Who?"

Jared rose from his seat, in effect letting her know he was done answering questions.

"Jared, who's the killer?"

"I've answered your questions. I've enjoyed our time together. I do hope you come again."

"Wait, Jared," Avery said as she jumped from her chair. "If I come again, will you tell me who the killer is, and why he's chosen his victims?"

"No, I won't. This is about me, not him... or her. You'll have to figure that out for yourself."

Just before he left the room, she threw out her final question. "Why does Mr. Phelan come to see you each month?"

Jared stopped his movement, still half inside and outside of the door. Turning to face her, he smiled before answering.

"That, Miss Avery Marie Grey, mother of a blue-tick beagle named Bailey, who's sound asleep in her purple princess kennel at 12714 Fawn Oak, is something you'll have to ask Bench. Good day, Avery, and be careful. There's a lot of sick people out there."

Slack-jawed, Avery watched as Jared left the room. He'd already known about Bailey, about her, and where she lived. She had no doubt he knew the killer, but he also had information being fed to him from the outside.

With shaking hands, Avery retrieved her notepad and pen, clicked off the recorder hidden in her bag, and slowly made her way to the closed and guarded door. She wanted out of that place as quickly as possible. She'd felt safe talking with Ramsey, but with one off-handed statement, she knew she just put herself in the hands of evil, and no exorcist would be able to rid this demon away. She was thoroughly screwed.

* * *

The Ranger and FBI operative stood behind the viewing glass in disbelief. When the warden had called to inform them of the interview, they decided to see if Jared fell for the pretty researcher. Would he reveal his secrets to the doe-eyed beauty? They got more than they'd expected.

"Good God," Dax uttered.

"No kidding. He gave her more information than we were ever able to get from him. More than what was disclosed in the trial. We need to go back and see what we've missed," Cruz stated.

"There was a lot of information to reconsider, starting with who his source is. Not only did he have someone stalking Avery, he called Joe... Bench. How would he know that?"

"Maybe something had slipped one of the times he'd come."

"No. According to the warden, Bench just sits there for one hour each month. He stares at Ramsey, never saying a word, not even when Ramsey taunts him. The warden said the only reaction Bench showed was on his first visit. He clenched his teeth. No, Bench is former Delta. He's been trained to not react to threats or taunts."

"Then we need to find his informant. It's a small list to sort through. My first guess would be a guard."

"Let's go see the warden. He can get us a copy of the interview. Thank goodness we had enough notice to get the search warrant signed."

The two men exited the observation room and joked about offering Avery a job.

"There's something to be said about a pretty face," Dax joked.

"Too bad it's not ours."

"Too bad."

CHAPTER 9

Avery tried to let her interview with Jared... No, Ramsey, not frighten her, but it was impossible. She'd planned on giving law enforcement a copy of her interview, even though the information was most likely not new to them. Ramsey had been so open, and why shouldn't he have been? Even if he'd implicated himself in other murders, his sentence wasn't going to change. Death row was still death row, not that he'd be executed anytime soon. In her research, she discovered most inmates stay on death row for over ten years. She also learned that death row and lifers were separated from the general population. They were isolated, even showering and eating alone. That left prison guards as his most likely informants. Who else could it be? Did anyone else have regular contact with him?

She had to double check her notes, but she believed she'd read he had Type 1 Diabetes. Wouldn't that require medical attention? Her father had Type 2, but he controlled it with diet and exercise. Was it the same with Type 1?

Unfortunately, Avery walked away with more questions than answers. She also walked away with some new leads.

Sadly, she had a rough draft due to Callum in two days. She hated working against a deadline, especially when there was a lot more to the story, but she needed the money. After taking a shower, loving on her dog and checking her email to see if there were any more threats from Bench, she finally sat down with her notes.

She wrote her draft with the facts, as well as direct quotes from Ramsey. She also included a list of questions she still had to research. For instance, she knew Hillary Phelan and the child's death was more than just random, it was pivotal to Ramsey's killing. This led her to question if the copycat was killing in pursuit of a sense of sick justice, or had Ramsey revealed his excitement of killing two at the same time? Had Ramsey sparked the killer to commit the crime on random victims, or did he target them? How did the copycat know Ramsey?

"Ugh! This won't work. I need more answers... Think, Avery, think!"

Avery dug through her bag in search of her recorders. She needed to thank her brother for the spyware... Not that he knew she had them. Just a few things someone could pick up by remaining silent, especially at family dinners.

"Son, tell me about your last arrest. Didn't you use a confidential informant?" Her father asked during one Sunday dinner months earlier.

"Yes, sir, we did."

"But isn't that risky?" Her mother asked.

"Not anymore than the CI would be any other time."

"Tell them about the pen, honey," Melissa prompted.

So he did. Avery learned all about spyware. How to put cameras in smoke detectors, how to use microphones hidden in fountain pens, and mini recorders that use WIFI, or in her case her hot spot, to immediately transfer the files.

Since she wasn't sure the internet and even hot spot

would be accessible, she used the fountain pen and saved it to her cloud storage. The more she thought about the day, the more she considered becoming a journalist. She felt a twinge of success in gathering intel, but she would contemplate her career choices later.

At the moment, her focus was on emailing her draft to Callum and prioritizing her next steps.

Two hours later, after hearing the swoosh of her email being sent, she pulled out new flash cards for her corkboard. It was time to focus on the copycat. Did his kills target a particular weakness or perceived sin?

"Okay, Avery, it's time to dig into victim number one's life. What sins are you hiding, Tiffany Flint?"

CHAPTER 10

Bench looked forward to having a new mission. Ever since he'd seen Avery at the prison, he hadn't been able to forget about her. It had surprised him when she recognized him. He'd changed a lot from his military picture that was plastered all over the news. That picture was from before he joined the Delta's. He was young and starry-eyed back then. There were no longer stars in his eyes. There was no longer hope. There was no longer love there either, at least not the romantic kind. He definitely loved his teammates and their families. Just thinking about Jacob, or Rocketman as Turbo's brother preferred to be called, tugged at his heart. Then there was Bama's pistol of a daughter. Bella was a year older than what Wesley would've been. That was the name he and Hillary had chosen. Would he have been as curious as Bella or as smart as Jacob?

'Nah, he would've been the best of me and Hillary, mostly Hil,' he thought.

His reminiscing was interrupted when Ethan entered the conference room where the Bravo team was meeting.

"I need everyone to clear their schedule for the next few months."

"Months?" Dodger asked. Most of their missions were short, a few days or possibly a week at most. To have one that long was new.

"Yes, months, at least for most of you. We've been asked to assist Knight Owl. The motorcycle club in Alaska is looking for the person responsible for the murder of one of their members who was killed here in San Antonio."

"This isn't the one who kidnapped Lola and Bella, is it?" Turbo asked. She was without a doubt the closest to Bama and his family. Bama had taken Turbo in when she was being hunted by the CIA, and their almost familia bond was obvious to anyone interested in looking. He'd become a big brother to Turbo and Jacob. So her reservations about the murder victim were understandable.

"Yes. Look, I know what you're going to say, and I agree with you, Turbo. The thug got what was coming to him, but the president of the Diablos was murdered yesterday, and the new leader is blaming the MC here for it. Generally we wouldn't care, but no one wants bloodshed in our town, even if it's MC blood. If they only killed each other, I wouldn't care. But a lot of innocent people could get caught in the crossfire."

"I don't see how we fit in though," their team leader Dodger said, then continued. "If we know who killed him and that it was most likely sanctioned by the former president, then why do they care?"

"We don't know that it was sanctioned. For all we know the former president was happy to be rid of the enforcer. What we do know is someone intervened in stopping Lola and Bella from being killed. This woman called Cruz and gave us Lola's location. Either there's a mole in the San Antonio MC, or there's an undercover agent embedded in their ranks. Cruz said no one was undercover at least to his knowledge. Either way, we have a group of bikers in our town looking for blood. Our job is to find the woman and bring her in, or at the very least give her a heads up," Ethan explained.

"What do we know about her?" Bench asked.

"Nothing of substance. Lola said she sounded like she was in charge and had ordered the enforcer around. She also said she didn't look like a biker. She was classy."

"That doesn't make sense," Archer debated. "Women are objects in the MC world. They have no say... not who'd be her old man, who'd screw her, or where she'd work. They are merely vessels, used and abused by the club members."

"How do you know that?" Turbo asked. "I mean, that's basically how every MC romance book presents them, but is it true?"

"I'm not sure what kind of books you're reading or how they portray them, but it's true. And how could women being used and tossed aside by multiple men be considered romantic?" Benched asked Turbo.

"Hey, don't look at me. I'm not the writer."

Ranger changed the direction the conversation was heading. As a former Texas Ranger, he too was familiar with the MC world. "This club isn't a pushover. Like Ethan said, they'll start a war just for the fun of it. They're part of the one percenters. Law enforcement has tried to infiltrate the club and bring it down from the inside. It would be a long play and I can't see a woman getting anything but screwed over, no pun intended. She'd have no voice, no power, unless..."

"Unless she's the President's old lady," Spud finished.

"Exactly. The President's woman would have control over the females, old ladies included. She'd be able to intimidate newly patched members or prospects, but not the established members. Think of it like the First lady. She has no direct power, but she has the ear of the man who does."

"Never underestimate the power a woman has," Ethan confirmed.

No one responded, but they all wondered if Ethan was referring to Kensley, his own woman who had recently moved in with him. She too was a force to be reckoned with.

"How do we find this woman? Are we going in undercover?" Dodger asked.

"I can do it," Archer offered. "I've been around MC's most of my life. My old man is or was, an enforcer for a club in Colorado."

"You were raised at the clubhouse?" Turbo asked.

When everyone turned and stared at her, she shrugged. "Romance novels, remember?"

"Well, there's nothing romantic about a club, and yes I lived onsite for twelve years, until my mother realized they were making me a prospect. She brought me and my brother to Texas. I think she was relieved when I joined the Marines."

"But former military still make up a large percentage of motorcycle club members," Turbo added.

"Geez, we might need to read some of those books for intel," Ranger joked.

"Not necessary. Archer, you, Bench and Ranger will take the lead. We're going to work out a plan. Turbo, you need to be a part of the meeting too .

"What about us?" Dodger asked, referring to him and Spud.

"You're too clean cut for this mission. I have another job for you two."

"Ranger's a pretty boy," Spud remarked.

"Well, thank you man, but I'm taken," Ranger said and pointed to his wedding band.

Ethan interrupted their potential sparring, explaining

Ranger would be working with Knight Owl Securities and the liaison for local law enforcement.

The group listened as Ethan laid out a mission plan. He was right about one thing; this would be a long play. Bench didn't mind, he needed to get involved in something other than worrying about Avery Grey and her incessant need to play with fire. He only hoped that her visit with Ramsey had scared her enough to drop her questioning. The last thing Ramsey needed was a way of entrapping her in his web.

CHAPTER 11

"The draft was great," Callum said shortly after she entered his home. "Though, I agree with you that more information is necessary. It sounds like your interview with Ramsey went well. You have a lot of direct quotes. Are you confident that you wrote them down word for word? The last thing I need is a defamation lawsuit from a convicted serial killer. That's not the kind of media attention I'd like."

"Oh, no, I'm sure. I recorded the meeting. I should've downloaded a copy of the files for your records. I'll do that when I get home."

"He didn't object to the recording?"

"I didn't ask, the recorder was hidden. I researched if there would be any legal ramifications for recording without his knowledge, but the rules don't apply to prisoners. Anything he says is admissible."

"Good thinking. Okay, now that I'm clear on the notes, let's talk about next steps."

"Okay." Avery was excited that Callum approved of her draft. She was worried it wouldn't be enough for him to see the direction she was going.

"You mention in your notes that all the victim's families agreed to be interviewed, with the exception of Mr. Phelan. Any headway in that area?"

"No, sir. He's made it clear he's not talking. He even sent me a cease and desist."

"But from your notes, it seems his wife's murder would have been a pivotal point in Ramsey's spree. Even though he wasn't able to finish his plan, he could've shared it with the copycat."

"That's what I think too. I can't explain how excited Ramsey was to talk about their deaths. I truly believe he shared that experience with the copycat killer."

"I agree. So, how do we get more information from Phelan?"

"I don't know, not without pushing him to take legal action. I have thought about stalking him. For instance, I know where he'll be on the twelfth of this month, and I know where he works. I'm just not sure we'll gain anything useful. Honestly, he wasn't even here when she died. I think my time is best served by looking for the copycat killer."

"Yeah, I'm torn on that. I believe there's more to Phelan's story than what we have. Will it help with this book? I'm not sure, but it's always good to have more information than to miss something that could be relevant. Also, I agree that you need to focus on the copycat, and I think you should visit Ramsey again."

"Really? I'm not sure he'll give me anything more useful. He will enjoy playing his games and taunting me if I go back."

"Explain."

"Well, he asked all about me but in the end, it was apparent he knew a lot more than I'd disclosed. This is why I believe he has a contact on the outside. I've put a call in to the warden about getting a list of his pen pals. Apparently, him being able to meet with me was unique. Most death row inmates stay in solitary confinement for twenty-three hours a day, with one hour outside for exercise. Mr. Phelan's monthly visits are typically a no-no. I'm trying to figure out how he managed to get approval. I'm assuming it's the same way you did. Wait, I'm not sure I even know how that happened."

"Oh, it's nothing. I've gotten to know the warden through the course of my various books and court appearances. He's been known to break the rules for me occasionally."

"Interesting," Avery said absentmindedly.

"How so?"

"Huh? Oh, I just find it interesting that the warden would do favors for acquaintances. That's got to be how Phelan got in. He must have some type of relationship with the warden. I'll have to dig around that, if it's even important."

"Will it lend anything to the storyline?"

"No, I guess not. It's just… well… if the warden breaks the rules about visitation, what other rules does he break? Could he be the leak? Or does he know who that leak could be? Could he be the copycat killer? Yeah, no, that doesn't make any sense. It's one thing to let a death row prisoner have guests, but to think he'd turned into a psychopath? Well, that's just ludicrous."

"All good questions. Don't ignore your hunches. You seem to be looking at this from an investigator's eye. I have no doubt that you'll close those links. So, do you want me to make another appointment with Ramsey for you?"

"What do you think? Will he give me any more information regarding the copycat?"

"Doubtful, but remember this book is about him, not solving a case. That's up to the police. Try to make him give you more information about himself. What motivated him to kill initially? Was it his childhood? Why the moral compass? And why did it fail to keep him from killing?"

"Oh, I think you're onto something. Yes, please see if I can get in to see him. In fact, see if I can see him on the twelfth. I might be able to kill two birds with one stone."

"Two for one."

Avery stilled. Had she mentioned that before? Did she write in her notes about her two for one deal with Ramsey? She must have. She was over-reacting. It wasn't a phrase only said by the serial killer.

'Two birds with one stone,' she silently scolded herself. She herself had said it. It was an innocent thought.

Noticing her demeanor, Callum looked at her quizzically. "Is everything okay?"

"Oh, yes, sorry. I was thinking about my next steps. If you don't have anything else, then I'll wait to hear from you about the twelfth."

"Sure, that's fine. Here's your first installment. I added a few hundred for getting me the document before the Friday deadline. Keep it up, Avery. You're doing a great job. I'm glad Angelakos recommended you."

"Me too," Avery said as she folded the check and placed it into her handbag. She was leaving Callum's office the same way she left the prison, with more questions than answers.

'At least this time, you're leaving with enough money to pay your rent. Get your head back on the job, and stop making assumptions that aren't there.'

Why would Callum be in contact with Ramsey?

'He wouldn't, you ninny.'

CHAPTER 12

Bench sat at the end of the biker bar and watched the foolish prospects. While he wasn't well versed in the biker world, he knew enough about being a greenhorn, and these boys were greener than snot. Where were their parents? Most of them were underage, and not surprisingly drinking more than their body weight. They didn't understand that being inebriated left them vulnerable. *'Stupid kids.'*

He'd been welcomed in as a prospect and understood their visit at the bar was a test. Archer had been patched in two weeks earlier. His family history and former military experience made him an easy recruit. There had been rumbling about the Alaskan MC being nearby, but no specifics about the feud had been broadcasted, at least not among the prospects. That hadn't stopped the kids from talking smack. As if his thoughts had brought his presence into focus, one of the kids approached him.

"Why are you way over here? Do you think you're better than the rest of us?"

"Nope."

"No what?"

"No, I don't think you're better. I know you aren't."

"Hey old man, you better watch what you say to me. I've been a prospect longer, so I have seniority."

Bench held his beer mid-air and looked the boy up and down. His slow perusal only ticked the young man off.

"What are you looking at?" The kid, who he found out was twenty, was cruising for a fight. The alcohol had made him think he was ten foot tall and bulletproof. Neither of those two were true. While he might have an inch or two in height over Bench, he wasn't bulletproof, and especially not against Bench.

"What's your name again?" Bench knew his name, but he was enjoying poking at the kid.

"Radar. And don't you forget it, Bench. You're a place for me to sit on. You need to respect your elders."

Bench nearly spit his beer out. "Elder, eh? How do you figure that? I'm nearly twice your age."

"Like I said, I'm the next to be patched. And when I am, you best watch your back."

Bench shook his head at the audacity of Radar's statement. The kid really did have a death wish if he was trying to push Bench around. It was time for him to leave. He'd given them enough to judge him by. However, Radar didn't agree. He pushed Bench back into the stool. That wouldn't have happened if Bench had wanted to stop him, and if the kid kept hounding him, he would shut him down.

"What you gotta say now? Are you ready to show me some respect? I think you need to call me master."

"Really? You want me to call you Master Bates. Isn't that your last name, Ronald Bates? Fine, I'll call you masturbate."

The other recruits were hanging on to their conversation, and began laughing at Radar's new moniker.

"Oh, burn. Masturbates. That's awesome, man," one of the recruits said, looking for Bench to fist bump him.

As much as Bench wanted to ignore the raised fist, he had a role to play so he bumped it. Radar however had recovered and tried to throw a punch, which Bench blocked.

Holding his fist still in his hand, Bench told the kid to go sleep off his buzz.

"You don't want to spar with me, kid."

"I'm not a kid!" Radar nearly screamed.

"Whatever you say. Now go away," Bench said as he released the recruit's fist, then reached into his back wallet for a few bucks to pay his tab.

Thinking Bench would be caught off-guard, the kid tried to punch him in the kidneys. However Bench had anticipated the cheap shot, and did a roundhouse kick thwarting his attempt.

The kid landed on the floor, spewing every curse word Bench had ever heard, including some really poorly made-up words.

"Help your friend," Bench told the fist-bump kid.

Turning his back to the group, he made his way to the door. Apparently, Radar had been roused by some of the other prospects and was still vying for a fight.

Sighing, Bench punched Radar in the nose, the break being heard by everyone in the bar. He looked at the other three wondering if they wanted to test him. Fortunately, common sense overrode their buzz and they backed down.

Bench pulled back to land another punch when he felt a strong grip on his shoulder. Spinning around, he came face to face with the club's secretary.

"Nice defense tactics. Learn that in the Army?"

"Nope. Learned it during my MMA fights."

"Really, how long you been fighting?"

"A few years."

"Do you have matches?"

"Yes. Usually a couple a month, depending on my work schedule."

"Let's meet tomorrow. I'd like to know more about your work and your matches."

"Sure. I can be there at three."

"Why three?"

"I have a meeting with someone tomorrow. It's not club business, it's personal."

"You'll learn that everything is club business, but I'll let it go for now. See you at three."

Bench nodded and left the building. He wouldn't let anything, not even an undercover gig, stop him from seeing Ramsey. No way would he let Ramsey think he'd lost his nerve or given up. No, this was non-negotiable, and probably something Ethan and Archer should know.

'Just get past tomorrow.'

* * *

Avery had arrived early, not knowing if Bench met with Ramsey at the same time every month or if it varied because of his work schedule. She'd already gotten approval to see Ramsey again. She still wasn't excited about the interview, but she knew that Callum's book would center mostly around Ramsey, so she had to make an earnest effort to get Ramsey to lower his guard.

At eight thirty, she watched as Bench exited his truck and greeted the guards. It made sense that they knew him, if he'd been coming every month for years.

She knew from her previous visit that he stayed one hour, and their meeting had been back-to-back. If he kept to the same schedule, he'd be out before ten, when her visit starts.

She'd spoken with the warden, and he finally agreed to provide a list of everyone who had written Ramsey a letter.

It was a crazy list, all women. What woman would correspond with a serial killer? She'd be happy to live her life without ever coming face to face with Ramsey, but she had a job to do. She had also been informed that aside from Bench, Ramsey's other visitor had been his attorney. Avery had done a quick search on the attorney and didn't find anything enlightening. She'd also spent the past three weeks reviewing court documents and digging deeper into the victim's lives. She'd discovered the third victim, Kelli Owens, was still having an affair after her boyfriend proposed. Her lover was never discovered. Avery wasn't even sure law enforcement knew about her extracurricular activities, but she wasn't unique. Adulterers were a dime a dozen, so why her? Same with the spousal abuser. How did Ramsey know about him? There were no hospital records. She had a hard enough time getting confirmations from the families. She understood people not wanting to speak ill of the dead, but eventually they admitted to their crimes, even if not illegal. Did he pick the victim randomly and then discover their sin, or was it the other way around? What about those he didn't find any dirt on? Did he walk away? He hadn't with Hillary, but was that a fluke? She had too many questions and wasn't sure he'd answer them, but what did she have to lose? Nothing but her innocence and sleep. She struggled sleeping for over a week after her last interview. She kept looking over her shoulder, thinking she was being stalked. However, she never found anyone acting suspicious. Ramsey had just gotten into her head. He could've had his attorney look her up, and he could have guessed that Bailey was a princess. He had a 50/50 chance that she'd be dressed in pink or purple. After their meeting, Avery changed Bailey's harness and donated her rarely used bed to an animal shelter.

Thirty minutes later she stepped out of her car and gave

the guard her documents. She noticed it was the same guard from her first visit.

"I'm surprised you came back. Are you going to come once a month too?"

"Ha, no way. I'm hoping I get everything I need this time. I'd be okay if I never come back here again."

"I don't blame you. I wouldn't willingly come here if I didn't have to. Just wait a few minutes, Joe should be done soon."

"How long has he been coming here? Since the murders?"

"No, probably only a couple of years. I know it was after he left the military, but I'm not sure how long that was. You'd be able to get that information, either from him or the Army."

"It's not important, I was just wondering."

"I have to say, I'm surprised Ramsey spoke so openly with you. I know the police were surprised too."

"Police?"

"Oh, you didn't know? Yeah, a Ranger and FBI agent were watching from the observation room."

"Are they here today?"

"I'haven't seen them, but they could've come while I was taking Joe back here."

"I wonder what they thought? I never heard from them."

"If I had to guess, they were happy you were able to get Ramsey to talk."

"Let's hope he does today."

Avery stopped speaking when she saw Bench exit the room. He slowed his pace when he saw Avery heading his way. She wanted to stop and talk to him, but it wouldn't be wise judging by the look on his face. She only hoped he didn't find her tracker. She'd picked up a small tracker that would provide her with real time data. It only worked within a twenty-mile radius. Once she was in San Antonio, she hoped to pick up his trail. She'd already done a trial run on her brother's truck, not that he knew about it. Sunday dinners gave her the opportunities to test several of her 'toys.' She was able to place the tracker and remove it after an impromptu visit that week to see her nephews. She'd been able to see everywhere her brother went, or at least the general area. Avery wondered why spouses didn't use this technology if they suspected their significant others were having an affair. Maybe it was a good thing she wasn't in a relationship. Lord knows he wouldn't like knowing how good she had become at using spyware.

"Mr. Phelan," Avery said when she came into his space.

"Avery."

She could tell he wanted to say more, but he shook his head and moved past her and the guard.

She however wasn't going to let it go. She couldn't. She might not get another opportunity.

"Say what you're thinking," she said to his back. She watched as he stopped and noticed his fists were once again opening and closing. She wondered if this was a coping strategy. Maybe it kept his anger at bay.

Bench turned around and walked close enough to Avery that she could feel his breath brush over her face.

"You're playing with fire. Ramsey is only going to give you enough to keep you hooked. He's not someone who does anything without a plan, and you're setting yourself up as his sacrificial lamb."

"And you? Are you his lamb too?"

"No, but you already know that." Bench shifted his attention from Avery to the guard. She knew he assumed she'd gotten his schedule from him, but she needed to protect her source, regardless of who it was.

"Would you believe me if I told you I've been following you? It doesn't take a rocket scientist, or a soldier to figure out when you come here each month. What I don't understand is why?"

"First, no I wouldn't believe you. You're too resourceful, and don't need to follow me. Second, my reasons for coming are my own. And you're right, it's not hard to see the pattern."

"But aren't you reliving your family's murder each time you come?"

When Bench didn't answer, she restated her question. "Would Hillary want you to face her killer every month? Don't you think she's forgiven you already?"

The tick in his jaw was all the response she needed to know that she'd pushed him too far. Bench blew out the breath he'd been holding, although she hadn't realized it since she too was holding her breath.

"I suggest you psychoanalyze someone else. Now, I have another appointment. Watch your back."

"From you, Bench?"

Again, the clenched jaw and contracting fists were the only obvious signs of his anger. He turned and walked away from her without answering the question.

"Good God, lady. You have some large balls. I've never seen someone push his buttons like that, not even Ramsey."

Avery wasn't proud of her taunts and attacks. She'd watched him stiffen when she asked about his wife. She knew she'd pushed him too far, but his self-control was impeccable. She wouldn't have been so calm if someone had attacked her... which was why she was sorry and owed him an apology.

'If he ever lets you get close enough to tell him so.'

CHAPTER 13

Bench punched the steering wheel. The nerve of that woman. She didn't know him, and yet she saw right through him. She knew he was punishing himself. That he'd never forgiven himself, much less think Hillary would.

The little interlude with Avery would make him late for his appointment. Of all days to run into her. He had no doubt she'd planned it that way. He should've just agreed to her stupid interview. There was so much he could never tell her, which was part of the reason why he'd declined her requests. He wasn't worried about her getting anything from the military, except that he'd been dishonorably discharged. Even though the discharge hadn't happened officially until his prison sentence was served. This kept her from assuming it had something to do with Ramsey or Hillary. So how could he excuse himself from missing her funeral, or not attending the trial? He couldn't. The fact was, there was a large part of his life he could never tell anyone about. Obviously Steve and Ethan knew, but no one else at ECP seemed to be aware of his former life. The guys had been surprised to hear that he was a widower.

He used the three hour drive back to disengage from his conversation with Avery. He needed to focus on his upcoming meeting with Axel.

"Axel. Go figure!" He muttered. Before he exited the truck, his cell phone alerted him to his mother's ringtone.

"Hey, Mom. What's up?"

"It's me, son. Your mother is arguing with the doctor."

"What's she doing at the doctor's?"

"We're at the hospital. Your mom thought she'd clean out the gutters without me being there. She slipped off the ladder and ended up breaking her arm."

"But she's okay?"

"Yeah, you know your mother. She's telling the doctor she only needs a sling and not a cast. She's driving me crazy."

"I'm glad you were there."

"I wasn't home when it happened. I drove up on the woman trying to wrap her arm with an old t-shirt and a spatula as a splint. Just make sure you never find someone like your mother. She thinks she's invincible! And don't get me started with her hard head. Us Phelan men are prone to find the most difficult woman in the room to catch our eyes. Well, except for Hillary. There was nothing stubborn about that woman, God rest her soul."

Bench took a deep breath. His parents had been talking about Hillary more often lately. At first it upset him, but they'd been right… She was a good woman, and she deserved to be remembered for more than her tragic death.

"Oh, she had her moments. You never saw how hard she could dig her heels in. She was stubborn about a lot of things, she just hid that side from you and Mom."

"You sound good, Joe. It's nice to hear you talk about Hillary. It's been a few hard years, but it's time for you find a way to forgive yourself. Hillary would want you to be happy."

Bench lowered his head. His father's words mirrored

what Avery had said to him. He wanted to forgive himself, but it wasn't that easy. While he was off protecting his country, he'd left his wife and child vulnerable and exposed to the evil nearby.

"I'm getting there, Dad. Thanks for letting me know about Mom. I'll try to get up there soon."

"No hurry, we know you're busy. Just know that we love you. Wait, your mom wants to say hello. Bye, son."

"Bye, Dad." Bench chuckled when he heard him tell his mother to stop harassing the nurse. "Talk to Joe instead." It was obvious his mother hadn't asked to speak to him. It was how his father had always been... a peacekeeper.

"Joey, oh I miss you!" His mother whined with her heavily Haitian accent.

Bench shook his head. No matter how many times he asked her to call him Joe, she refused and said he'd always be her little Joey. "In my mind, you're still that five-year-old boy who sat at the end of the bar, begging to lick the bowl when I made cookies."

"I hear you've been causing trouble... again."

"Psst, don't listen to your father. He makes up stories. It's really nothing. I was okay fixing it myself, but oh, no, your father insisted that I go to the ER."

"Mom, you know you can't fix a broken bone at home."

"Would you have stopped and gone to the ER if you'd broken a bone while in Afghanistan?"

"That's different. There's no ER on a battlefield."

"Well, if a man can suffer through the pain, a woman would just flick away any discomfort like a fly."

"Discomfort?"

"Yes. Have two large boys without any painkillers, and then come back and tell me that a small break is a pain I can't endure."

His mother always brought up her delivery experience

with both him and his brother. It was always a losing battle after that point.

"I know, Mom. Why didn't you wait and have John clean the gutters when he got off work?"

His brother and family lived three blocks from his parents and was always available to assist them, not that they ever asked for help.

"You know Johnny is a busy man. If the city isn't calling him out at all hours of the night, then Sara has a list of things for him to do."

"I'm sure he's kept busy. Murder doesn't happen in an eight-hour shift."

"You sound just like him. Both my boys are putting themselves in danger... Still. My heart stopped beating while you two were in the military, and now... you both put your life on the line every day. Why did Johnny have to become a detective? And don't get me started on you."

"I know, Mom. Look, I have an appointment I'm late for. I'll call you later and see how you're feeling. Breaks hurt worse the second day."

"Okay, Joey. I love you. Please be safe."

"Always."

Only Bench knew that wasn't true. His safety had never been first on his list. Hanging up with his parents reminded him that he needed to take some time off to see them. New Orleans wasn't a far drive... It was just scheduling the time. With this new assignment, he didn't know when the next time he'd be free to go see them would come around. Looking at the dashboard clock, he sighed and opened his truck door, only to come face to face with Radar. Both eyes were black, and white surgical tape was adhered to the bridge of his nose. Yep, he'd broken the kid's nose.

"You're late."

"Actually, I'm right on time. Take me to Axel." Bench began his walk toward the clubhouse, not waiting on Radar.

The smell of sex, cigarettes and liquor hit him first when he opened the door. Then his eyes settled on the large bar, where three half-dressed women sat around a large biker. One was in his lap and the other two were practically straddling both thighs. The man looked up, nodded, and resumed drinking from his shot glass.

'Well, Archer's not suffering,' Bench thought.

In truth, he wouldn't want to be in Archer's place. He knew the barflies would be part of the cover, but he hadn't been involved with anyone since Hillary's death. He'd had the occasional hookups, but there were no relationships, and never a second hookup. He avoided any kind of attachment.

Axel walked out to meet Bench. There were no handshakes or greetings, just a simple head nod to an empty booth.

"Want something to drink?" The waitress asked when they settled in.

"No, Doll. I'm good."

"Don't come back unless I tell you too, LeeAnn." Axel's tone was dismissive and harsh. Bench wondered once again why women thought motorcycle clubs were romantic.

"Do you know why I wanted you to come see me?"

"You said it was because you wanted to know about my job."

"When we patch someone in, we have them work at one of our businesses, generally a legit one. There are a few occasions where it's more profitable, either financially or in information, for a member to work outside the club. We have a lawyer and doctor that work out in the real world."

"Makes sense."

"It would also make sense for you to stay at ECP."

"Really, now that does surprise me. Do you know anyone there?"

"No, just their reputation. ECP could help us expand our business."

"I'm not sure I understand."

"If you stayed working there, you'd be able to get intel about possible raids, perhaps drug dealers who are no longer in operation. You know, places where we could slide in and take-over the businesses."

"You do realize that we typically hunt guys like you down for prosecution."

"In some cases, but if they start looking into us, you'd be able to give us advance notice."

"So I'd be, what... a double agent?"

"Sure, if that's how you want to see it."

"You said this was for patched member, but I'm still a prospect."

"True, but I think you'll become patched sooner than later... before Radar."

"He's all bluster. I'm not worried about him."

"Not after watching you last night. You said you're part of a fight club. I see this as an additional opportunity. First, we could have inside information for betting purposes, but we could also use the club for money laundering."

"You've given my resume a lot of consideration."

"I do with each prospect. Some are money cows for us, while others are the perfect grunts. What do you say? Are you interested?"

"Let me make sure I understand everything. When, or if, I'm patched in, you want me to continue working at ECP and feed you leads. You want me to continue with my MMA fighting and give you betting odds so you can launder the club's money."

"Exactly, except we want you to do this BEFORE becoming patched. Like I said, I need to see if you add value as a member."

"And how long would this probationary period last?"

"Let's say six months. If after then, you can opt to stay a prospect, or leave with no trouble from us."

Bench lifted his eyebrow at the offer. He'd have to ask Archer, and possibly Turbo, if an MC would let a prospect leave without retribution. Sure Archer had, but he'd been a kid.

"I think that's reasonable. Are you expecting me to check in daily? Because that's not always possible. If I'm on an assignment, it's not likely I can make a call and check in."

"Bench, I've done my research on you. Your family was murdered while you were on an assignment with the Army. And you spent some time in prison."

Bench growled. He didn't know who Axel's source was, but that information was supposed to be sealed. In fact, as a Delta, the transcripts were to be destroyed. He'd have to have Turbo check into Axel's background. His link with the Army had to go up the chain pretty far for that clearance.

"And?"

"And I know you're not someone that would follow directions. Just like today, you told me what time we'd meet. There's not a prospect out there who would've done that. But I'm not offended... That's exactly the kind of recruit I like. Insubordination is a plus sometimes."

"Good to know. I'd have nothing but A pluses if that was the case."

"Probably so. For now, what I'll tell you is that we won't manage your time. We'd rather you be working with us, not for us. If later you want to leave ECP, then we'll figure out what you can do for us. But for now, I'd only ask that you contact us with leads. You're always welcome at the clubhouse, and to the extras available here," Axel said as he nodded his head over to Archer and the fourth woman who'd captured his attention.

"Sure."

"So we understand each other?"

"Yes. And I'll call you directly?"

"For now. Later on I might have someone else become your handler."

"He doesn't seem to be busy," Bench said, nodding over at Archer.

"He's still learning the ropes, but it's possible in the future."

Bench stood from the table, offered his hand to Axel, and confirmed he'd call when he had some information. As he walked by Archer, one of the ladies reached out and tried to draw him in.

"Where you going, big guy?"

"Nowhere. Do you think you'd be able to pull yourself from him?"

"Hey, Prospect. I have plenty to share. Take a seat."

Bench sat two seats over from Archer and understood why Archer hadn't left his barstool. He had a perfect view of the clubhouse from the bar's mirrors. Looking at Archer through the glass, he tried to hold back a chuckle. Archer wasn't enjoying himself, despite the relaxed stance he'd adopted.

Bench stayed at the clubhouse another half-hour before climbing back into his truck. He'd not missed the death stare coming from Radar.

Using his car's Bluetooth, he called Ethan and gave him an update.

"If you don't need me, then I'm going to head back home."

"Go on. Be safe at your fight tonight," Ethan said just before he disconnected the call.

Even Ethan had figured out his pattern. He'd obviously gotten lazy about hiding his actions.

'Some Delta you are. Leaving breadcrumbs for everyone to find. Even a nosy researcher.'

CHAPTER 14

Her assumptions had been correct. Ramsey said nothing. He'd sat stoic during all her questions, so she left early. The three-hour drive had been a waste of her time, except for seeing Bench. Even now, six hours later, she felt horrible about the accusations she hurled at him.

She'd followed him to a warehouse on the Southside. There wasn't any signage, but there were ten or twelve motorcycles sitting outside. She'd sat there for nearly an hour before he walked out.

His next stop was to his apartment. It was a cute complex with single garages and a patio space for each unit. There weren't any flowers or color outside of green to brighten up his place. He lived in a middle-class neighborhood. She wondered if his neighbors knew about his wife. Not that it mattered, or should have. She just couldn't see him attending block parties, or putting up Christmas decorations.

She hadn't planned on a long stakeout, and she was getting hungry. Just when she'd decided to leave, figuring he was home for the night, his garage door opened. She could've waited and let the tracker lead her to his destination, but she wasn't sure how long the battery would last on the device. So she pulled in three cars behind him. Twenty minutes later, he pulled into another large warehouse, but Gym was etched on the siding. What kind of gym was he going to? It looked sketchy, but there were a lot of cars, most of them expensive. It couldn't be too rough.

She sat there wondering if she could enter the gym without alerting him to her attendance, especially since she continued to see people stream in. She wasn't dressed to visit a gym. However, when two women passed her, she decided to join in beside them, hoping going in a group would lessen her visibility. They were not dressed for the gym either. Instead they dressed like they were going to a dance club.

She took advantage of the girl's conversation, and gathered enough to know this wasn't a typical gym.

"He's supposed to be here tonight. I only bet when he's fighting," the blonde said.

"Because he's gorgeous?" Her friend asked.

"Well, there's that, but Bench Press has never lost a fight. And if he was hurt, I'd be the first one to offer him mouth to mouth," the blonde giggled.

"What do you think he does for a living? I can't see him selling insurance. With a body like that, he has to do something physical."

"Oh, can you imagine him in low-slung jeans, with a carpenter's belt slung just as low? He'd be shirtless and holding a power nail gun. I bet he would know what to do with that gun."

"Or maybe he's a plumber and offers to fix your pipes." The girls moaned with their mental images. Avery nearly moaned too, thinking of Bench shirtless and wielding a large tool.

When the door opened, the man ushered the three in without any questions.

The large cage was centered in the room. People were standing around the enclosure. Some were drinking beers, others were handing over cash, and the girls were all close to the fence. Avery however, stayed in the background. She didn't want to catch Bench's eye. She wanted to see what he did after hours, and then go home and fantasize about his large pipe.

'Gawd!'

Fifteen minutes later and the announcer called for everyone's attention. The two fighters were introduced, along with their stats. The girls were right, Bench had won every fight he'd been in. They also were right about how drool-worthy he was shirtless.

When he turned his back, she nearly cried at the tattoo on his left shoulder blade. A black photorealistic image of a woman nestling a baby against her chest was so detailed she recognized Hillary's features. There were no names etched in his flesh, but the lone tear dropping from Hillary's face said it all. She could feel his loss.

As much as Avery had decided to leave after Bench began his fight, she couldn't. His body was a work of art. The muscles and sinews moved gracefully, and willingly followed Bench's direction. His opponent really hadn't had a chance. The fight was one-sided, and unfortunately not in the other man's favor.

The blunt kicks to the man's jawline, the jabs at his kidneys, and the blood that sprayed the girls in the front, they all told a story... Bench's story. How many of his strikes had to do with his wife's death, and the monthly visits to see Ramsey? Did he fight other days, or was this a regular match? She continued to have more questions regarding Joe Phelan, or Bench as she'd come to think of him. He didn't look like an average Joe. His nickname fit him better.

When the announcer called the fight and declared Bench

as the winner, Avery took it as a sign to slip out of the building. Since she knew he'd be in the arena for some time, she walked over to his truck. As she was extracting the device from under the rear bumper, she stopped in her tracks when she heard a very pissed off Bench demanding answers.

"Did you really put a tracker on my truck?"

What was he doing outside? He was supposed to be talking with his fans or taking a shower... not catching her with her spyware.

"Actually, you don't have to answer that. It would probably be a lie anyway. Are you that determined to get an interview that you'd follow me?"

Slowly, Avery turned to face the still shirtless man. She couldn't help but watch as his chest moved up and down with his restrained breaths. She allowed her eyes to travel down his pecs, to his abs, and then the magical V that men work so hard to attain. Well, for the record, he had met that goal. When he growled out her name, she quickly lifted her eyes to meet his and forgot what his question was.

"Avery! Why are you following me?"

Oh, now she remembered why he was mad. What could she say that wouldn't make her sound like a stalker? Nothing.

"I know you're mad, and you're right, it was wrong."

"I'm beyond mad. I thought I'd made it clear that I do not want to answer your questions. I'm wondering if I should get a restraining order."

"No, Bench, that won't be necessary!" Avery hadn't meant to nearly yell her response, but the last thing she needed was her brother knowing she'd been stalking an innocent bystander in her attempt to make a name for herself as an author.

"Bench? Where did you hear that?"

"Um, well... I've heard it from a lot of people. It didn't

seem to be a secret. The Ranger or maybe the FBI guy told me, and then Jared Ramsey said it, and then tonight your fighting name was Bench Press."

Bench hadn't responded to her rambling. She wondered if Ramsey felt as uncomfortable as she did under his condemning stare.

"I'm sorry. I had no right to invade your privacy. I won't do it again, I promise."

"You think saying that you're sorry is enough. Tell me why I shouldn't call the police? You do know you broke the law, right?"

"Well, I'm not one hundred percent sure that's the case. I mean, don't you do some things that would be questionable with your job? Well, I'm just doing my job. Really, it's not very different."

"Oh, really? Well, let me educate you. I'm chasing criminals, kidnappers and sex traffickers. You are chasing a story, and I've made it abundantly clear that if you continued to harass me, I'd report you. So tell me how your job is anywhere close to mine?"

"If you put it that way, it sounds bad."

"And you have a way of spinning this in a good way?"

"Um, no, I guess not."

"Instead of calling SAPD, I should call your brother and let him take care of you."

"You wouldn't dare!"

"Oh, I'd dare. How do you think Texas Ranger Grey would feel knowing you were stalking a source for a story you're not even publishing? You're a researcher, not an author."

'Ouch that hurts,' she thought. It wasn't a lie, but talk about low-blows.

"Are you tracking me any other way? Are my phones

tapped? Did you put surveillance cameras facing my front door?"

"Don't be ridiculous."

"Right, because it would be far-fetched, says the woman holding a tracking device, which was probably bought on Amazon."

Again, he was right. She'd been excited to find it online, even with free shipping, it was a win/win.

"Fine. I promise I'm not tracking you with anything else."

"When did you put it on my truck?"

"This morning."

"You left after me."

"Yeah, well, I was there a couple of hours early. When you went inside the prison, I placed it inside the bumper. I lucked out that your bumper was chrome. It wouldn't have stayed in place if it had been one of those plastic thingies."

"So glad my truck met your criteria for spying on me."

"This is getting ridiculous. I've promised to not follow you again. This is the only device I was using to keep tabs on you. I won't call, text, or email you ever again. Can't we just chalk this up as a learning experience?"

Bench's jaw clenched, just as it had when she confronted him at the prison. Recognizing this, she knew she owed him another thing.

"I also want to apologize for what I said to you this morning. It wasn't my place to question you or your motives. Geez, Bench, I've never acted so impulsive like this before. I've only been focused on getting this research right. It could affect my career if I can get it done to the author's satisfaction. I really am sorry, though. I know I crossed the line with you."

Bench watched as Avery averted her eyes from him. He knew she was sorry for her earlier comments, and for getting caught tonight. But would she have been so contrite if he hadn't discovered her? It really didn't matter at that point. He wasn't going to call the police, or even her brother. He just wanted to scare her, and he believed he had.

"Thank you for the apology. I'll let this go if you swear to leave me alone... To not follow me." He couldn't imagine what would happen to her if she'd followed him to the clubhouse. Had she?

"How long have you been following me tonight?"

"Um, maybe five hours?"

Cursing, he knew she'd seen him at the clubhouse. Did he really believe she wouldn't have gone looking for him there? Nope, not at all.

"Listen to me, Avery, and I'm dead serious."

"Okay," she tentatively said.

"My job requires me to meet with... Well, let's just say they aren't civilized people. You need to stay away from the location you followed me to tonight."

"You mean the warehouse with all the motorcycles?"

"Yes, that's exactly what I mean. You have to promise me that you'll not go there for any reason." When she didn't immediately agree, he growled. "Promise me, Avery. This is non-negotiable!"

"Fine, I promise."

"I'm not joking. If I see you anywhere near there, or just following me in general, I will call your brother."

"Okay, I get it. I won't follow you anymore, and I won't go to that shady warehouse ever again."

"Or here."

"Why not? It's a gym. I saw the equipment."

"It's not the kind of gym women like you would join."

"Women like me? What do you mean?"

"It doesn't matter. Just stay away from here, and every other place I haunt. Got it?"

Nodding, Avery agreed.

"Now, get in your car. I'll stay and make sure you get in unharmed."

"Or you're staying to make sure I leave."

"That too."

"Okay. And for whatever it's worth, I really am sorry. I went too far, I know that."

"Go, Avery." Bench didn't need to hear any more of her apologies. He needed her out of his business, especially with the MC job in the works.

"Bye, Bench." Avery waved and walked back to her car, not realizing that someone else was standing outside, overhearing their conversation. If she had, she'd recognize him immediately, and she'd be able to identify the copycat killer.

Slinking back into the darkness, he watched as Bench slapped the tailgate of his pickup truck, cursed the woman, and walked back into the gymnasium.

CHAPTER 15

Avery had taken Bench's threats seriously. In fact, when she told her friend about that night three weeks later, Janie nearly blew a gasket. She'd received another lecture on stalking, and not to mention the financial and legal trouble Avery could've found herself in. So for three weeks she'd not tracked him. She'd tried to put that night behind her. She was no longer fixated on Bench, giving her time to dig into each victim's life, and then compare it with the copycat killer's victims. There hadn't been a lot of information reported on the kills, but she'd gathered enough to write a draft for the first eight chapters. When she'd presented them to Callum, he'd been happy with the research, and the flow of the manuscript.

The worst part was that within those three weeks, two more murders had been credited to the River Walk copycat killer. The death toll had jumped to five.

The five however did have a commonality. They were all taken from the south side of town and strangled at the River Walk. Or perhaps they'd been killed, and then staged at the River Walk. Either way, they were all taken from dance clubs or restaurants. Also, all five were women. Since these didn't seem to follow the same logic as Ramsey's kills, there had to be something that the police weren't sharing that linked them, besides the fact that they were found at the River Walk. But what?

She had posed her suspicions to Callum during one of their meetings.

"You've studied serial killers and their reasons for murdering. Besides the whole '*my father hit me,*' or '*my mother never loved me,*' excuses, what other reason would cause someone to kill so many people?"

"There's a lot of reasons. As for the copycat, I'd say he's looking for the attention. He's copying Jared, but still making it true to himself. For instance, they are all women, dressed up for a night of dancing or attracting the eyes of available partners. Also, if your suspicions are correct and he kills them before going to the River Walk, it makes the kills unique for him. So, he's really only a partial copycat."

"Then it's not about Ramsey. He wants his kills to be seen, and what better way than doing something that will gather the public's attention? He could have left his victims at the kill site, but would they have been discovered? And if so, would they all be linked to him? But by tapping into Ramsey's moniker as the River Walk Strangler, he's ensuring his kills don't go by unnoticed," Avery surmised out loud.

"Exactly. I really think you're onto something. What do you do now?"

"Well, I'm not going to get anything else from Ramsey. I've exhausted that source. I've spoken with the families of all the current victims, trying to see if there's a link, aside from their attire and locations. They were all last seen on Thursdays, but I'm not sure if it's even relevant. But I've not found anything that would connect them with Ramsey. Have you noticed that the last three victims looked like they could be my sisters? They all have my brown hair and brown eyes. Don't you think that's scary? I mean, the first two were blonde, but these last three kills were after I first met with Ramsey. Do you think there's a correlation?"

"It could be a fluke. Like you said, the first two were blondes. It could be that his MO hasn't changed, just the availability has made him choose brunettes. And statistically, brown eyes make up forty-five percent of the population in America."

"Yeah, I didn't know that, but it makes sense. Is that number real?"

Chuckling, Callum told her about his last researcher who had gathered a lot of random facts for future references.

"Do you think you have enough information to complete the manuscript?"

"I don't know, Callum. I feel like I need to pull a few more strings and see if it helps me learn more about the copycat."

"Just remember, you're not here to solve a crime. I agree there's a lot we could learn about a copycat killer, and it might add some value to the book. Just don't lose sight of the goal... or the deadline."

"I won't. I think it's time for some field work."

"Avery, please tell me you're not going to do anything dangerous."

"No, I'm not stupid, nor do I want to die, but wouldn't it be interesting to go to a few clubs and see if I find the same person also frequenting these establishments? It's just a thought."

"Just be careful. It's a good lead, and you're right, you'd be able to attract him better than me... But do you really want to attract a serial killer?"

"Well, I don't want to go on a date with him. I'm just thinking I'd do some observing. I've learned a lot over the years by just fading into the background. I'm not the kind of person who'd immediately draw someone's attention, and I'm okay with that."

"When do you think you'll do this field work?"

"Well, like I said, all five victims were last seen on Thursday nights. For a lot of clubs, Thursdays are ladies' nights. So, in three days."

"Okay, but I want to hear from you Friday morning. If I don't, I'll call the police."

'Seems like threats of calling the police have become my new norm.'

"I promise. Until then, I'll work on the revisions you just gave me."

"It's a plan."

Avery left Callum's home feeling like she was finally making some traction with her research. She'd call Janie to see if she would like to join her for a girl's night out.

CHAPTER 16

Avery had enjoyed the evening with Janie, but unfortunately she'd not seen anyone suspicious. They'd gone out the following Thursday, much to Janie's displeasure.

"I'm out of town next week. Promise me you're not going to do anything stupid, like go to a club alone."

"Geez, do you realize I have to promise someone nearly every day to not act stupid? I know what I'm doing. You've been the last two weeks with me and we've not seen anyone that gives us the heebie jeebies."

"But each time it was to a different club. I just don't want to worry about you."

"I promise I won't go back to the bars we went to. Now go and enjoy your conference. Maybe you'll find yourself in someone's briefs."

"Har, har. It's not like that's the first time I've heard that lawyer joke. I'd never date another lawyer, we're too competitive. We'd spend all our time trying to best each other. No thanks."

Avery said her goodbyes and looked at the calendar. Next Thursday was the twelfth. Even though she promised to not stalk Bench, it hadn't stopped her from fantasizing about him. She'd wake up from a hot and heavy dream at least four times a week. Images of him on a large Harley, with nothing covering his torso than one of the motorcycle club's cut. Then there was the reoccurring dream of him wielding a large hammer and all sweaty, which made her wonder why the thought of a sweaty man was enticing. Outside of her dream world, she'd never want to do the nasty with a sweaty and smelly man. *Too many romance books.* But her favorite dream was of him in that fighting cage. Only instead of him kicking some other dude's butt, he'd trap her against the fence. His hard core would be crushing her soft chest. One of his large thighs wedged between hers, and one hand would be holding her hands above her head. His other free hand was making her body shiver with pleasure. Each morning she'd awaken hot and fired up. Even Bailey had moved from the bed. She'd found her sleeping on the sofa. Apparently, her dreams came with a soundtrack.

Maybe she'd go to the club around the corner of the gym next Thursday. She wouldn't see Bench, but just knowing that he was there could lend itself to new dream material. Of course, she could go in and watch the fight. Just because it was the twelfth didn't mean he'd be there. He could be on another job. She wouldn't know unless she went inside.

Grabbing a pint of Ben & Jerry's Half Baked, Avery asked for Bailey's opinion on the matter.

'You promised.'

"No, Bailey. I promised to not follow him. If I just show up because I'm in the area, then that's just a bonus."

'Sure, justify it all you want.'

"Excellent! I'm glad we are in agreement. Good chat, Bailey."

CHAPTER 17

Bench threw the jab, not seeing his opponent. He never saw his opponent. He only saw *him*. He always saw *him*. He lived every day seeing the glint of victory in *his* eyes. He saw the satisfaction gloating from the man. Bench's bloodlust was only meant for one person. Was the man satisfied knowing he'd killed not just his wife, but his future? No, Bench knew he'd merely been caught, not sated, and definitely not repentant.

It wasn't until he had water splashed in his face did he realize the referee was trying to pull him off his opponent. Snapping immediately out of the trance he'd been in, Bench raised his hands, letting the referee see he'd stopped.

It wasn't uncommon for MMA fighters to get carried away. It wasn't uncommon for them to be in the ring because of demons haunting them either. No, none of that was uncommon. Bench's anger however was contained in all aspects of his life, until that bell rang. It was as if his brain switched from being a good and respected member of society into the homicidal maniac he ached to be.

"Geez, Bench!" his promoter yelled. "I won't be able to

book you any opponents if you kill them all. Take a breath. Get some air," Ricardo yelled over the crowd, who were either cheering Bench on, or booing him. He deserved their boos. No one should cheer him on.

Nodding, Bench left the cage, grabbed a bottle of Gatorade and pushed open the exterior doors leading into the alleyway.

'What is wrong with you?' Bench always wondered this question, but he knew the answer. It was the same answer every day. *Revenge.* Revenge he'd never been able to exact. If only he'd been in town when his family became the eighth and ninth victims of serial killer, Jared Allen Ramsey. If only...

Bench turned his attention to the car parked a few feet from the streetlamp. He could see movement, but he hadn't really been paying much attention. Then he heard the scream.

"Hey!" Bench yelled out as the man was attempting to shove a woman into the trunk. Bench dropped his drink and sprinted toward the idling car.

"Let her go!" he yelled as he gathered his speed and was within fifty feet away.

Either it was Bench's quick arrival or his size, but the man dropped the woman unceremoniously on the asphalt and sped away.

It was the anger in the woman's eyes that stopped him from kneeling before her. His instinct was to triage her and then pursue the kidnapper, but the vixen wasn't crying, or clinging onto his safe arms. No, this vixen, Avery Grey, was spitting mad.

"Why did you do that?" she demanded, quite loudly.

"I just saved your life, lady. Why are you pissed at me?"

"I didn't need you to save my life. I was just fine on my own."

"Did you hit your head on the trunk? You know, the trunk that man was trying to shove you into."

"Get out of my way," she replied, still with venom.

When she stood, he watched as she pulled her skirt down, pushed her hair out of her face, and looked him up and down. So he returned the favor.

Bench tried to make sense of the crazy woman. Oh, he'd known she was nuts, but would she go this far for a story? She was dressed like a hooker. Tight mini skirt, a barely there shirt tied under her ample breasts, and stilettos that made his body think of sin.

"You were trying to get thrown in a trunk?" No way could that be true. Who wanted to be tossed into a trunk, carried to God knows where, and treated like... well, a prostitute?

He shouldn't have cared. He'd done his good deed for the day. Perhaps it would make up for the poor guy he'd left moaning on the mat.

She ignored his question and began muttering, "Now what? Who knows if he'll try again? God, I can't believe this happened!"

"Did you get hit in the head? Do you need a doctor?" That was the only explanation Bench could grasp at for her questions.

"No. I'm fine. I just need to get to my car and come up with a new plan. Geez, I was so close."

Bench wanted to walk away from her, but manners had been drilled into him from his mother and grandmother, then the military. So when he offered to take her to her car, and she seemed to hesitate, it made him wonder if she really had banged her head.

"You have no problems getting tossed in the trunk by a deranged serial killer, but you're leery of me driving you to your car... by the man who saved you from being tossed into said car."

"*Fine,*" she pouted.

She walked in silence to Bench's truck. He then offered his hand so she could lift herself up into his pickup, which surprisingly she accepted.

The four-block ride continued in silence. Bench didn't know what to say. He'd never known someone who was upset by not being kidnapped. In his line of work, the ones they rescued were thankful and grateful for their quick thinking, but not this woman.

"Thank you. I'm sorry I yelled at you. I've just worked so hard trying to get a lead, and now I've got to start all over."

Avery opened the door and exited the truck. Bench stopped in front of her, stopping any forward movement. Instinctually, Bench pulled her close enough to whisper in her ear.

"You drive me crazy," he growled.

Stunned, Avery looked up trying to understand the meaning behind his words. Only she was met with something stronger than anger. She saw interest, sexual interest. Did she make him crazy because of her stunts, or was it because he desired her? She didn't get to ask these questions, not when he grasped her around the neck and crashed his lips against hers. It wasn't a gentle kiss, nor was it an explorative one. It was one out of anger, frustration, and raw emotion. She didn't let him back away. She wrapped her arms around his neck and opened for him to take the kiss deeper. She could feel his restraint, and wondered what it would take for him to let go... To fully give himself over to the kiss.

She knew he was physically engaged in the kiss, his body told her so, but why her, she wasn't sure. She also wasn't sure she wanted the answer.

Bench hadn't kissed another woman since Hillary. He might have had sex, but he never kissed the women. But he couldn't have stopped himself even if he'd tried... not that he had.

Her moans drove him even further, pushing her back against the truck door. Pinned in, she took advantage of their closeness by wrapping one of her legs around his thigh. He could feel her heat throbbing for attention. He hiked her leg up higher, running his palms up and down one thigh.

"Bench," she moaned when their lips separated.

It was as if she'd thrown cold water on him. He moved away, rubbing his temples and muttering to himself. He'd not steadied her with his quick extraction. After righting herself, she tried to reach for him, but he stepped further back.

"Bench?" Avery asked with sincere concern.

"I can't do this. You're too risky. I can't..." But he didn't have to finish his thought. Avery understood clearly enough. She was a risk-taker. She was driven, and she intentionally put herself in harms way. She didn't like it, but she understood. She wasn't even mad... Turned on, yes, but not mad. It was what it was... She was nothing like Hillary.

"It's okay. Don't worry about it," she said as she righted her dress once more and began to walk to her car. Bench couldn't lift his head to watch her leave, nor could he apologize for the kiss.

'Right, it was more than just a kiss.'

He looked up when she called his name from a safe distance.

"Thanks for saving me tonight." She gave him the most brilliant smile he'd seen in a long time, then waved goodbye.

Shaking his head, he reminded himself this was the same woman who'd stalked him, tracked him, and followed him to the prison. She was out of her mind. He wanted nothing to do with her type of crazy.

'Yeah, keep telling yourself that.'

All he'd done was think of that kiss while trying to sleep.

Could she stay out of trouble? At one point, he seriously thought about calling her and agreeing to the interview. He knew she'd jump at the opportunity, but he'd be doing it for the wrong reason. He didn't want to talk to Avery about Hillary. Those two needed to occupy different places in his head. Hillary's memories were surrounded with love. But Avery, well, it teetered between lust and frustration. One made him sad and regretful, while the other drove him mad.

When his father had said the Phelan men go after strong, stubborn women, his mind had instantly thought of Avery Grey. He'd never met someone so relentless.

'Be glad she's not your woman.'

Only the thought didn't make him happy. In fact, since she'd met him, his days consisted of short tempers, clipped tones and sexual frustration. She needed a warning sign; *'Approach at your own risk.'*

Grumbling, Bench turned on the morning news, dreading his day. He'd met with Axel three days earlier and given him the odds for his fight that week. His part of the mission hadn't been too difficult, unlike Archer's. Each time he walked into the clubhouse, women were draped all over him. They'd spoken that week, but he'd not learned anything useful. He was too new in the club to ask questions about this mystery woman. However, the barflies had no problem trashing those of their sex. When he inquired about the President's woman, the girls evaded his questions. Whoever she was, she scared them. Now, a month and a half into the assignment and he'd still yet to meet the woman. Bench and Archer were coming up with their own speculations about the mystery woman. They needed proof to support their assumptions.

His thoughts stopped when something on the news caught his attention. Avery's smile was mocking him.

"Avery Grey, one of San Antonio's foremost aspiring

authors has disappeared and is feared to have fallen victim to the River Walk Strangler copycat murderer."

Despite the reporter continuing with his broadcast, Bench sat on his sofa knowing two things.

One, he would hunt for Avery Grey, and shake her until her brain lodged itself back into place. And two, he would find this copycat killer, and do to him what he'd never been able to do to Jared… exact his vengeance.

This copycat would wish his fate was the same as Ramsey's. But this serial killer wouldn't die by lethal injection. This one would die by Joe Phelan's very own hands.

PART II

CHAPTER 18

Avery's head hurt. Had she had too much to drink at the club? The last thing she remembered was kissing Bench... Then his rejection. Of course she would remember that, clear as day. She didn't remember driving home. She tried to rub her eyes, hoping it would make things clearer, but her hands were restricted with the zip ties.

'Great! Now I remember.'

Avery looked around the room surprised. She wasn't in some basement or storage building. She was resting on a full-size mattress, not the creepy, filthy ones she'd seen on television. No, this one had sheets, a down comforter, and Euro pillows.

'What the bejesus? Has Martha Stewart kidnapped me?'

The bedroom door was ajar, so she hadn't been locked in. Tentatively she stood up and slowly opened the door and peered from side to side. She could hear a man humming and pots and pans clinking. Unsure how to proceed, she opted to keep her presence unknown, at least for the time being.

The hallway led into a large family room... one that she

recognized. He'd had her meet him there once to review her notes.

Softly she called out to Callum, unsure if it was just the two of them.

"Ah, you're awake. Come and have some coffee."

Standing still and not moving, he sighed and led her by her bound hands to the kitchen table.

"What am I doing here?"

"Research, of course." When she failed to understand, he elaborated. "You told me you were going to do some fieldwork. After not having any success, I thought I too would do some research. I wanted to know how easy it would've been to capture you. Actually, it was extremely easy."

"I don't remember seeing you at the bar."

"I wasn't. I parked my car beside yours. When you stopped to search for your keys, I put a chloroform handkerchief over your nose and lifted you into my car."

"Why are my hands bound?"

As if noticing them for the first time, Callum chuckled. "Sorry about that. I wanted to see what your reaction would be to waking up with them on. Here, let me cut them."

Once they were removed, Avery rubbed her marred wrists. The bindings weren't too tight, but her hands were swollen because of their restraint.

"I want you to use this data however you see fit. There were a couple of things I learned. First, the capture has to happen fast. Your first reaction was to fight me when I placed the handkerchief over your mouth and nose. I would assume that should be expected. Second, I could see the value in having a partner. Of course, it wouldn't be necessary, but it would provide support, as well as an alibi. The last thing I learned was how easy it was to target you. You were oblivious to your surroundings. Perhaps it was the alcohol you drank, or your false sense of security since you were out with your friend."

Avery sat at the table and tilted her head, trying to take in everything he'd said.

"I thought you said you were waiting by my car. Was it you who tried to put me in the trunk?"

Callum didn't answer, instead he simply leaned against the bar sipping his coffee and not losing eye contact.

"Um, Callum. You're scaring me. I think I'd like to go on home now. I still owe you a revised draft."

"Yeah, I've been thinking about that. I think you should work from here. I should've said so before. It just makes more sense."

"No, Callum. I want to go home. I need to take care of Bailey. I'm sure her bladder is about to burst." Avery rose from the table, eager to leave.

"Sit down!" Callum yelled.

With trembling limbs, Avery resumed her position. She'd never had bad vibes from Callum before. Had she missed something?

"What's going on, Callum?"

"Oh, nothing. I just think our arrangement should change. Besides, who's going to miss you? No one knows about your project, right?"

Janie knew but she wasn't about to drag her into this frightening and unnerving situation.

"No, of course not. I signed your NDA. But I still have family dinner each week, and like I said, I have Bailey."

"I'll have someone take out Bailey."

What kind of out was he taking about? Out to use the bathroom, or out as in dead? Either option caused her body to shiver. She didn't speak and couldn't maintain eye contact. His body language seemed casual, non-threatening, but his words were not comforting or light. They were downright scary. She'd wanted to ask him a question for months, but had been holding it back. At this point, she didn't have anything to lose.

"Callum, how come you didn't use your previous ghostwriter?"

"Hmm, I was wondering whether you'd ever ask. It really is a tragic story. Kelli got engaged, so she had to go."

"I don't understand. How is getting married a tragedy?"

"Well, dear Avery, Kelli had a fiance and a lover. She had to choose one, and well, she chose poorly."

Avery tried to process what he hadn't said. There was something about this situation that was gnawing at her, then it all clicked.

"Kelli Owens," she whispered.

"That's right. She should have made the right choice. It really was too bad."

Avery looked at Callum with a new understanding... a terrifying understanding.

"It was you. You were the River Walk Strangler." When Callum didn't debate her statement, she continued. "But what about Jared Ramsey? I don't understand."

Still silence from Callum.

'Think, Avery.'

"He was set up. You set him up to take the fall. Then why did he confess? They found all the souvenirs at his house."

"Was he innocent?" Callum finally asked.

Avery rubbed her temple, trying to piece it all together. The first seven were linked through their perceived sins, but Hillary was random. These copycat kills are random. It was impossible for Ramsey to be the copycat. Her eyes shot up. She didn't even try to hide her fear.

"You're the copycat killer. Did you kill Hillary too?" Avery had so many scenarios running through her head. If Callum was the copycat, then when did he start? Hillary was the only variable. Had Ramsey been Hillary's killer, or was it Callum?

"No, it was Ramsey. Right?"

"You really are a great researcher, Avery. I knew you would eventually find the truth."

"Were you killing together? You were. That makes sense."

"Go on..." he instructed.

"You could've stopped when Ramsey was caught. You could've gotten away scott free."

"Had you ever wondered if there were similar killings outside of San Antonio? There are other highly visible tourist traps all over the country."

"You never stopped, you just changed location. And now you're back. Why?"

"Why do you want to be an author, Avery?"

The change in subject confused her, but she knew he was getting to a point.

"I like weaving a narrative, and it's a creative outlet." Then she understood. Just like writing was an art to her, his deranged mind thrived on expressing himself through fear and death.

"I too, like to weave a narrative. I'm the hero and the villain in this story. Who do you think turned Ramsey in?"

"He was caught accidentally."

"Was he?"

Avery wasn't sure what was true anymore. The man who she worked so hard to impress, to validate her writing, was a cold-blooded murderer. And now he had her trapped. She knew what her fate was, so she decided to get some answers to her burning questions.

"What do the five recent kills have in common? They're all women, but they vary in age and physical appearance."

"Unfortunately, the police withheld a key clue from the

public. You see, when I saw how excited Ramsey got when killing Hillary, it made me reconsider my subjects."

"Subjects?"

"Sure. I needed test subjects to see if I could emulate the same emotion Ramsey had experienced."

"But they weren't pregnant, so you chose random victims."

"Yes and no. They were random to some degree. I mean I didn't have any personal link with them, but they were all pregnant."

"What?" Avery gasped.

"Yeah, the police neglected to inform the public. They could've warned pregnant women all over the city to be alert to the danger."

"They couldn't have been too far along, otherwise it wouldn't have gotten by the press."

"You really are talented. The police never drew the same conclusion."

"That being?"

"Each victim was killed in the order of their pregnancy. Ashley had just discovered she was pregnant thanks to two pink lines. Erin was about eight weeks along. Crissy was 3 months. I think you get the picture. Each one begged to let them go, to save their child, just like Hillary had. I could've picked up where Ramsey had left off. But I wanted to build up to taking a nine-month-old baby's life."

"You're deranged."

"Perhaps, but I'm methodical. It really is kind of clinical if you think about it. All except the last two could've had an abortion. In fact, I was pretty sure Ashley and Erin were planning on it. I just saved them the emotional distress that they would eventually experience."

Avery remained silent, tracing the wood grain in the table with her recently painted nails. She'd been so stupid and naïve. Everyone warned her to stay away from this story, but she knew better. She'd never intentionally put herself in harm's way, or so she thought.

"I'm not pregnant."

"Not yet."

Avery shot her head up. She understood his intentions. He was going to impregnate her only to kill her and the baby.

"You should think of this as a promotion. My next target is six months. I can either wait until then, or perhaps I'll let you carry the baby full-term before I complete my goal. That really depends on you."

"Callum," she whispered. "You don't have to do this. You're an intelligent, handsome man. What happened to you? How did you get involved with Ramsey?"

"That, my love, will have to be a discussion for another day. I have some errands to run. I'm leaving you here, but let me tell you the specifics of your house arrest. We are off the grid in the hill country. There's no town or neighbor for miles. The doors and windows are all rigged to blow. If you try to exit through them, you'll not survive. And while you may think that's a better fate than living here, think again. I have a meeting with Janie today. She's concerned about you, and knew you were working with me. Imagine my surprise when she called and asked to meet with me. I could always make her number six and you seven, eight, or nine. I thought about taking her anyway, just to make sure you behaved, but that would give the police an unnecessary link. But I will... if you push me. Then there's your sister-in-law. Did you know she was four months pregnant? No, I didn't think so. She and your brother were keeping that a secret until Thanksgiving. We could have a little family party. You, Janie, and Melissa. I'd only need one more to round out the numbers."

"Please, don't hurt them. They're completely innocent. I'll stay put."

"Good girl. Now I've left a laptop in your room, along with all of your notes and drafts. You need to finish what you started. Obviously there's no internet or way of reaching out to someone, but it will fill your days while I'm gone."

Avery couldn't have responded even if she'd known what to say. How had she missed the signs? Were there any signs? She hadn't thought so, but there must have been. Was he on the police's list of suspects? Not likely. She'd worked right beside him and never suspected his sickness. No, this wasn't a sickness... it was evil, debased, obsessive, and methodical.

"Well, if we're done here, I'm going to go meet your best friend. There's nothing in the house to use as a weapon. All the utensils are plastic, as is the dinnerware. I'm sure this won't be the first time you've eaten off paper plates. There's microwavable food, so there's no need for pots and pans. Besides, those would be a painful weapon if you lobbed one at my head."

Callum smiled that grin she'd once thought was cute. This just proved once more that a pretty face could hide evil lying beneath it.

"I'll see you tonight. We have some work to do."

Avery had to find a way of escaping. No way did she want to be inseminated by a serial killer. If she hadn't been scared to death, she might've laughed at the situation. She'd not had sex in over a year, and now a murderer was planning on bedding her.

'Over my dead body.'

But she knew she wouldn't take her own life, not if it meant her family was in danger, not to mention whomever he'd replace her with. If she killed herself, she'd be responsible for the death of another woman.

CHAPTER 19

Bench sat across from the Bravo team, telling them about his past. The only one not surprised was Ethan. He saw empathy from the men and tears from Turbo.

"You should have told us," Ranger said. "When my daughter died at her mother's hand, I kept it to myself, but it changes you, or it did me."

"Man, I don't even know what to say," Archer added.

"What can you say? I've tried to move past all the pain, but it's not been easy."

"Or successful," Ethan added.

Bench nodded. Ethan had been right. He hadn't successfully moved past Hillary's death. He kept going to visit her killer. He reasoned it was to make sure Ramsey never forgot, but that wasn't true. He didn't want to ever forget. Ramsey wasn't remorseful, the only one hurting was Bench. Wasn't that what Avery was trying to tell him?

"Avery should be our focus right now. I can't change what happened to my wife and son, but I can save Avery."

"I'm going to be frank here, Bench. It might be too late to

save her. All we know is that the victims were taken on a Thursday and their bodies were found on the following Sunday. How long they were alive we don't know. The coroner might give us that information, but I'd reach out to Dax before getting mired in the weeds," Ethan suggested.

"I can call him and get some answers," Ranger offered.

"Good. Now, Archer, what's happening with the MC? I think you'll need to stick with that mission and let us handle Avery."

"I get it... I don't like it, but I understand." Turning his attention to Bench, he continued, "I'll be a phone call away. This MC mess is a long-play, but I've got you."

"Thanks, Archer. I'll call Axel and tell him I'm on a mission and unavailable. I can't divide my focus, Avery comes first. She's the one in imminent danger."

"Agreed," Ethan said.

"Now, Turbo, tell me everything you can about Avery's life."

"Well, Bench probably knows more than I do right now. I'll dig, but he's been gathering intel on her for months."

Bench shook his head, bewildered how Turbo knew, but he'd discovered that hackers were more threatening than any spook, and even stealthier.

"She lives alone with a dog, Bailey. Her brother is a Ranger. You might know him, Timothy Grey. Anyway, he's married with a child. Her parents are a typical middle-class family. Her best friend is a lawyer, Janie Oliver, and was with her the night she'd been taken. I'm meeting with her in an hour, and I'll see if she will come here to meet with the group. Avery's been working with Callum Easton on a research project."

"The author?" Spud asked.

"My wife is a huge fan of his work. Willow says it's like he gets into the killer's mind and draws the reader in.

Personally, I've seen enough death to last me a lifetime. I sure don't want to read about it for entertainment," Dodger replied.

"She's doing research for an upcoming novel about Ramsey and the copycat killer. That's why she'd been stalking me. She wanted to talk about Hillary's death. And now I may have been the last one to see her."

"Explain." Ethan stated.

"Last night I stopped someone from tossing her into his trunk. We had words. She wasn't happy with me when I dropped her off at her car."

"Did you see her actually get in her car?"

"No." Bench slammed his fist against the table. "She pissed me off and I drove away."

"Okay, let's do this. Archer, you go to the clubhouse and we'll call if we need you to come in. Turbo, you do a deep dive into Avery's history and this author. He might be able to fill in some of the holes in this story. Bench, get the best friend in here, and Ranger you contact Dax and Tim and see what they have. Explain Avery's link with ECP and that we're taking on this job with or without their consent. Dodger, you and Spud need to go talk with this author. I don't have to explain how time sensitive this is. Avery's life is on a timetable, and we're not sure what that table even looks like."

"What about you? I know you have something brewing," Dodger asked his father-in-law.

"I'm going to find out what the warden knows, and hopefully get in to see Jared Ramsey. We all have the same goal... hunt for Avery. We're not focusing on solving a crime. That's for the police to handle. Avery is our one and only mission. Are we clear? Everyone know what their job is?"

When the group all nodded their heads, they cleared the conference room and went to work.

Before Bench left the office, Ethan pulled him aside. "Are

you okay? This has to be bringing up a lot of emotions for you."

"I've spent the last five years blaming myself for not being here to save my wife."

"And now?" Ethan pressed.

When Bench didn't respond, Ethan did. "You blame yourself. You think you could've stopped this from happening if you'd have given her that interview."

"Or if I hadn't driven away before she got in her car."

"What about the other seven families she met with? Did those interviews stop her from being taken by a killer?"

"No."

"Then this is not your fault, just as Hillary's death wasn't. It's time to bury your self-imposed guilt. It's not helpful to anyone, especially not Avery. Do you get me?"

"Yes, sir. It's just a garment I've worn for years."

"Would have and could have are part of being human. Yet none of those could've changed the outcome. Get your head on straight, we needed to hit the ground yesterday. Since we can't, we will go full speed starting right now."

"Yes, sir. I'm going to drop by Janie's house. I don't want to give her a chance to decline my request."

"Smart thinking. We'll reconnect when you get back."

"Thanks, Ethan. Telling the team about my wife, my prison sentence, and my link to Avery wasn't easy."

"I know, son." Bench chuckled at his endearment. There was only a ten or twelve year difference in their ages, but Ethan treated everyone on his team as if they had all been under his protection, much like a father would.

After a hard back slap, Bench left ECP's office realizing he felt a little lighter knowing his friends had his back. However it didn't absolve him from leaving Avery vulnerable. He had to trust the team to help him find her.

'Just like your Delta team tried to be.' His thoughts had been doing that a lot lately... berating him for his stubbornness.

He was done being a solo artist. He was part of a team, and he'd not forget that so quickly.

CHAPTER 20

Avery walked back into the bedroom she'd awakened in. She noticed a suitcase sitting in the corner. Had Callum gone and taken clothes from her house? Tentatively, she approached the bag. What if it wasn't clothes? What if it was a trap?

"Just open the bag," she instructed herself.

Slowly she unzipped the case, lifting it a couple of inches. When nothing jumped out or went boom, she pushed the top over. They were clothes… her clothes. Callum had been in her house. He'd seen Bailey. Did he kill her? Her sweet Bailey was her baby. She couldn't think about her poor girl, not when she had other problems to worry about.

As she dug through the case, her fingers touched what she thought was cardboard. Instead, they were polaroids. Resting on her calves she had to stifle her yell when she saw the images of his last five victims. She immediately knew how the police were able to tie them together. Each woman had a slice through their belly, as if an old-school cesarean had been performed. Resting on the open wound was a pregnancy test. The viewing window was red, not pink. It was red with the victim's blood. Tossing the pictures aside, she fled for the bathroom, only making it to the sink. Callum was clearly deranged. He'd emulated Hillary's death. Two for one, just like Ramsey.

She had to get out of there.

"Think, Avery. Use that big brain of yours."

She remembered doing some research for one of her college essays on the various emergency management systems available. There had been a huge debate on whether someone could access a 911 dispatcher through text messages and laptops without access to the internet.

"Gawd! I can't remember what it said to do or even if the FCC approved it." It had been years earlier. She remembered researching the subject but not the conclusion was on the project.

Avery began scanning the laptop's start menu to see if there was even that option, especially since she was using a Mac. Apple had been years ahead of Microsoft when it came to tracking and communicating with others. Could she remotely access her cell phone? They were both Apple products. Could it be as simple as a find your phone option? If it was, could she piggyback on the internet or cellular service to reach out for help?

"Only one way to find out," Avery said as she opened the app and selected 'find my phone.' When the wheel continued to spin, she tried to think of other options.

If a pay phone could call 911 without coins, surely the same technology was there for phones, smart or analog. But what about for the hearing impaired? How would they contact the police? Wasn't some type of hardware required?

She wasn't a tech-savvy person, so she opened the settings file, typed in TTY and was directed to the accessibility icon. Both TTY and RRT were options. Unsure what the acronyms stood for, she typed in 911, hoping the call would connect. When it continued to spin, and then an error popped up directing her to turn her wireless service on, she tossed the laptop onto the mattress.

"With all the technology we have, surely there has to be a way of contacting 911 without internet service," she growled out.

"If I get out of here, I'm going to learn how to hack into computers. What is this world coming to? We are so reliant on the internet we can't even ask for help without it... not even the deaf."

"I can't even Google a solution!" She yelled to no one. She had no doubt Callum had bugged the room, if not with audio, definitely with video. She was trapped and he knew it.

Avery stood and looked out the windows. Callum hadn't been bluffing, there were wires interwoven through the windowsill. The sun was still pretty high in the sky. When would he return? And more importantly, how was she going to handle it when he did?

Avery hadn't ever been one to cry, especially if the tears weren't going to help her out of a situation. If she'd have been pulled over for speeding, then some tears might possibly sway the outcome, but no amount of tears would change her fate. If anything, it would just make her head hurt, and she needed it clear.

Assuming that Callum would check her keystrokes or use some other way of monitoring her activity, Avery did a hard reset on the system. This wiped out her saved story, and any of her notes Callum had downloaded for to use.

'Have fun trying to trace me now.' The thought prompted her to stick her tongue out, in the event Callum was watching her remotely.

CHAPTER 21

Bench was surprised to come face to face with Callum Easton when Janie opened the door.

"Mr. Easton, you were next on my list to contact."

"Mr. Phelan, I wish I could help more, but like I was telling Janie, I've not seen or heard from Avery since last Friday when she turned in her latest notes."

"I was going to see if Janie would come to ECP with me. Our team will be able to gather as much information at the same time, instead of me having to relay everything. Mr. Easton, you should come too."

Janie nodded. She'd do anything to find Avery. Bench hadn't missed the tears still pooling in her eyes, or the red tipped nose she kept dabbing with tissue.

"If you think it will help, then sure. I've always been interested in seeing the interworking of your company. The word on the street is quite favorable, even a little hero-worshiping. I can follow you. Janie, would you like to ride with me?"

"It's okay. I'll take my own car."

"Janie, I suggest you accept a ride, either with Mr. Easton or myself. You're not in any condition to drive."

When she hesitated, he pleaded.

"Fine. I need to take Bailey out first."

"Bailey? She's here?" Bench asked.

"Yes, Avery's dog. When I went over this morning, the poor thing was beside herself. I brought her home and figured I'd give her to Avery when she got home. It wouldn't be the first time I took her. She's pretty loveable for the most part."

"She didn't like me," Callum laughed.

"It was strange. She kept smelling him, as if she was familiar with the scent. When Callum didn't take her to what the source was, she wouldn't quit barking."

"More like howling," Callum stated.

"And pulling on his pant legs. I've never seen her act like that. She wasn't happy he wasn't doing her bidding," Janie stated.

"It's the breed. My parents have a bloodhound and he's relentless when he's got a scent he's tracking. I've literally seen him walk into a glass door trying to follow the scent," Bench said.

"That's Bailey."

"I can take her out if you want," Callum offered.

"Are you sure you don't mind?" Janie asked. She wasn't sure Bailey would be as willing as Callum seemed to think.

"Sure, we'll become quick friends."

"Very well. Mr. Phelan, could I have five minutes to clean up?"

"Absolutely, and please call me Joe."

"Thank you, Joe. I'll be ready in a couple of minutes, for sure by the time Callum is back with Bailey."

Both men agreed. Bench offered to walk with Callum. He'd like to have a conversation without Janie listening.

"Mr. Easton,"

"Callum. Please call me Callum."

"Okay, Callum. I stopped a kidnapping last night. Avery had the grand idea of taunting the killer. Fortunately, I was outside, saw it happen, and was able to thwart it. She promised to not do something so stupid again."

"She's rather aggressive when it comes to her work."

"What you call aggressive, I call stupid. You've researched this sicko. Do you believe she's still alive?"

"It's hard to say. He could have already killed her, and is just waiting till Sunday to dispose of her body. That was one of our working theories... that he killed early and planted the bodies later," Callum said.

"That's one of ours too. One of my associates is working with the Rangers and FBI to get the TOD for the other victims. The time of their deaths will give us some insight, hopefully."

"The other theory we were kicking around was that he or she had a hit list of some kind. She was looking into the other five victim's lives to see if she'd missed anything."

"She did the same with the River Walk Strangler. That's how we met."

"Yes, she told me you refused an interview. She was pretty persistent."

"To say the least. Do you think she was taken because I refused to do the interview?" Bench knew it was unlikely, but he needed absolution.

"Absolutely not. The copycat had already killed two or maybe three victims before she began her research."

"That's what my boss told me too. It's just two people I personally know have been targeted by a serial killer. It's a little eerie."

"I can only imagine."

The two men walked in silence while Bailey continued

her sniffing before she finally found a spot to relieve herself. Once again, she immediately went to Callum, sniffing his pant leg, sitting and looking up at him for directions. When he failed to give her one, she began growling.

"That was a complete one-eighty." Just as Bench had said it, Bailey continued her growling and added tugging at his pant leg, as if she was trying to get Callum to move.

"I guess she's ready to go back inside," Callum chuckled.

Janie met the men at the door and extracted the leash from Callum.

"Let me just put her in her kennel. I keep a spare one here for when Avery and her have a sleepover." Janie's voice broke when she said her friend's name.

"We're going to find her," Bench reassured.

"I hope so… but I'm not so sure she'll be alive when you do. Avery said the killer follows a pattern. I can't lose her."

"Me either," Callum stated as he pulled her into a side hug. Again, Bailey was not happy with him.

"He's jealous, too," Bench noted.

"It's so not like him. I mean, we've not had a lot of men in and out of her life, but she's always curious, but I've only seen her act like this once before. I guess she's more sensitive to Avery's absence than I could've imagined."

"Dogs," Callum stated, and started walking toward the door.

"Do you want to ride with us too?" Bench asked the writer.

"No, I'll drive my own car. I have a couple of errands to do before I go home."

Bench assisted Janie into the truck and waited for Callum to pull up behind him. Ten minutes later, they pulled into ECP's front parking lot. Visitors never went through ECP's back entrance. As it was, the front had a rarely used conference room, a set of bathrooms, and a receptionist desk. All the work ECP did was behind the metal door, away from the general public. There wasn't even access to their upper floors from the front office.

"Not what I was expecting," Callum said disappointedly.

"We don't open the guts of our business to the public. This is where we meet clients, families, and usually law enforcement."

There wasn't a receptionist at the desk, at least not a human. The video cameras alerted the team whenever someone entered the building. At that point, someone would come and welcome the guest. This particular day, Gunny was the one to greet them.

"Ethan knows you're here. He and the others will be joining you shortly. There's drinks in the conference room's mini fridge if anyone would like one."

"Thanks, Gunny," who simply nodded and entered the required code and palm print to enter the company's epicenter.

"Now that was impressive. Palm scanners? I can't imagine what you keep locked behind those doors," Callum said.

"It's just another means of ensuring our clients' problems remain private."

"What kind of client's would you need for that level of security?" Janie asked. She'd put on her attorney hat, making her just as curious as Callum had been.

"We work with a lot of law enforcement agencies, the DEA, FBI, CIA, and local police departments. There's always sensitive matters that need to be kept from prying eyes."

"Well, wasn't that tactful," Ethan said as he reached over and shook Callum and then Janie's hands. "I'm Ethan Clark. Please have a seat and when the rest of the team arrives, we can go through what we have so far."

One by one the Bravo team entered the large room. Gunny then showed Special Agent Cruz and Ranger

Chambers into the room. After all the introductions were made, agreeing to use first or last names only, Ethan opened the floor. This would be the first of several meetings that afternoon. The team wasn't going to give their guests too much information. This was going to be a one-way intel swap.

Cruz began the questioning. "Callum, when was the last time you've seen or spoken with Avery?"

"Last Friday she met with me. It was a scheduled meeting. She was turning over some of her notes. We didn't usually talk during the week, only on those scheduled days."

"And you, Janie?" Dax asked.

"We talk just about every day. She was determined to uncover the copycat killer, despite my pleas. She'd figured out that the victims had been taken on Thursdays, which is typically ladies' night at the clubs. We went together a couple of times. Then last night we went, but we left early, or at least I thought she had too. But Bench, I mean, Joe told me he came to her rescue last night around midnight. We'd left around ten. Avery is very hard-headed, and she must have circled back after we left."

Bench scoffed, then nodded for Janie to continue.

"Well, it's true, but there's a reason for it. She's always trying to prove herself to her family. Don't get me wrong, they're great people. They just don't appreciate all that Avery does, and they minimize her career choices."

"What about her former finance?" Cruz asked.

"She doesn't speak to him ever! Jeffery treated Avery horribly. Of course, her parents couldn't look past the MD after his name to see how he treated their daughter. Eventually, she stood up for herself and walked away from the relationship... Not that her parents ever let her forget it."

"Is there any chance he's involved in her disappearance? Maybe we're just assuming it's the copycat," Callum stated.

"Possibly," Cruz mused. "We'll look into that avenue, but for now let's assume our original theory is correct. Please continue, Janie."

"So, we went out last night. It was a typical night, minus the fact that she was looking for a killer. Anyway, around ten we closed our tabs, and said our goodbyes. She was parked on the other side of the road."

"Do you think there's a chance she went back inside?" Ethan asked.

"Sure. It's exactly something Avery would do." Janie couldn't hold back her smile. "Avery has always been a ball-buster with everything she does. Except when it comes to her family, and for a while there, Jeffery."

"Did you find her car?" Callum asked.

"It was still at the bar. From what we can tell she never made it home," Dax answered.

"Oh, my God," Janie cried, covering her mouth with her hand. "I can't believe this is happening."

"We're going to find her," Bench once again promised.

"Callum, can you share with us what research Avery has turned in?" Cruz asked. "In fact, we'd like a copy of it."

"I'd have to check with my publisher. This is all for a book that I've already received an advance for."

Bench growled at Callum. Turbo patted his forearm, reassuring him that she'd get the information either way. When he met her eyes, she winked. Heck, she could already have it as far as Bench knew.

"You do what you have to do. If necessary, we'll get a subpoena," Cruz shot back. That made him good people to Bench. Her employer shouldn't be playing the legal card... Not when time was of the essence.

"I'm sure that won't be necessary, but I'll call him once I get out of this meeting. Trust me, I want to make sure she's safe, just as much as you all do."

Bench looked over at Janie, who was shooting death glares toward the bestselling author.

Good, Bench thought. He didn't want them to confide in each other and leave ECP out of the loop.

"Well, thank you for coming in, Callum. I'm sure we'll be in touch," Cruz said as he stood up and walked him out.

"Janie, please let us know if you hear anything from Avery or her family. You never know, the smallest thing could blow this whole case wide open," Dax stated.

"I will. Thank you all for looking for her. It's nice to know there's even more people looking for her. She means everything to me," Janie said through her tears.

Bench let the group know that he was dropping Janie off, and would be right back to continue the meeting.

"Genni can take her, if that's okay with you?" Ethan offered.

"I can take her," Callum offered.

Bench might've missed the stiff reaction she'd had if he hadn't placed his hand on the small of her back to escort her out of the room.

"Nah, you said you had errands. We'll make sure she gets home," Bench answered.

"Okay, if you need me for anything, just give me a call." Callum exited the front door, pulling out his cell phone before he even made it to his luxury car.

"Can I just wait here until you're ready?" Janie asked. She wasn't sure why she trusted him, but she did. Perhaps it was because he tried to stop Avery's earlier abduction, or maybe it was because of Avery's crush, not that she'd ever admit it. Janie's job was to read people's words and body language, and Avery's interest in the super soldier was obvious.

"Sure."

Ranger stopped Janie from leaving when he called her

name. "Why did you really not want Callum to take you home?"

Janie wasn't sure if she was being ridiculous, but she answered his question honestly.

"I don't have a reason... it's just this feeling. I know this will sound stupid, but he just gives me the creeps. It's like there's something he's hiding, and I don't think it's about the book."

Motioning for her to resume her seat, Cruz asked her to elaborate.

"As an attorney you develop a keen sense for honesty. You learn to read body language, but more importantly you listen to what they aren't saying. What they're holding back."

"And what is he holding back?"

"Okay, I'm going to tell you everything I know. I wasn't comfortable talking in front of Callum, but Avery wasn't a researcher for him. She was a ghostwriter. She was doing all the work, researching and writing the entire book and getting absolutely no credit. He had her sign an NDA. As her legal representative I reviewed it, and for the most part it was a standard document, but there was some language that now has a chilling and unsettling meaning for me to ignore."

"Such as?" Ethan asked.

"It was like he took an NDA and a Last Will and merged them. There was verbiage about all files, recordings, and videos were to be turned over. So I wasn't too concerned about that, but then it said something to the effect that in the event of her death, all royalties originally negotiated would not be passed on to a person of her choosing or the executive of her legal will. Typically, with royalties, they are paid to any survivor outlined in their will for seventy-five years. Even though she wasn't going to be named as the writer, she would still be listed as a researcher and collaborator. As such, she was given a percentage of the royalties. Granted it wasn't a large percent, but why state the two percent would revert to him? Also on the NDA, she was given very defined instructions on what she could and couldn't tell others. For instance, the fact that I even knew about the NDA would've been a breach. However, as her attorney, I had full understanding of the document. I don't know, it's really nothing that would put a target on his back. I've read too many NDAs to know what is normal and what's not. If I hadn't looked over it, it would've felt normal to Avery. She signed it regardless of my unease, but I kept a copy. I can get it for you guys if you want. But other than that, it's just a feeling."

"In the military, and I'm sure it's the same with these two officers, your gut feeling can mean the difference between life or death. You'd be hard pressed to convince anyone in this office that a feeling is irrelevant," Bench replied.

"Thank you."

"Anything else?"

"Okay, I know this is going to sound crazy, but then there's Bailey."

When the group looked confused, Bench informed the group that Bailey was Avery's dog.

"She's a beagle, and her nose has led her into one problem too many. Anyway, she usually sniffs a visitor and goes about her business. She's a very friendly and love-seeking dog. She'll fake a hurt paw and give whines of distress for a little attention if she feels ignored. Quite the show girl. However, the minute Callum entered the room, she ran to him, sniffed and sat in front of him. You have to understand, I've only known her to do this once before with Jeffery. He was mad at something and to punish her, he locked Avery out of their house. Bailey hadn't always been a fan of Jeffery, kind of like Callum, but when he was around, she could smell Avery on him, and it settled Bailey down. Only that one time when he locked her out. Bailey began tugging on his pant leg and nearly bit him when he didn't let Avery in. The only thing we could figure was that she knew Jeffery had been around Avery and wanted him to take her to Aves. She stood by the door waiting for him to let her outside and when he didn't move, she started growling, barking and scratching at the door. It was the most aggressive I've ever seen Bailey, and well today, how she reacted around Callum raised the hair on my neck."

"She did that with Callum while we were outside. She practically bit his leg when she didn't seem to get his attention. I saw it for what it was, jealousy, but you could have something there. She wasn't in distress when I held her, and she was overly friendly," Bench added, thinking about the wet kiss she'd given him when he picked her up and carried her the rest of the way back into the apartment.

"Before you came, she'd gone nuts, which was why I had to kennel her. She kept trying to get Callum to take her outside, as if he could lead her to Avery."

The men nodded in understanding.

"I know this sounds crazy. Maybe I'm just looking for trouble where there isn't any."

"We want to know everything. Like I said, the smallest thing could bust the case wide open," Dax replied.

"Do you know Avery's brother, Tim?" Janie asked the lawman.

"I do, and so does Jack," he replied, then nodded over to Ranger.

"Will y'all keep him in the loop? He's a good guy, but his parents irritate me. They never treated Avery with any bit of respect."

"Yes, we will. He's at his parent's house hoping there will be a ransom. I will tell you, none of Avery's family knows about her work with Callum," Dax answered.

"Not surprising."

When Ethan nodded his head, Bench excused himself and returned a couple of minutes later with Genni and Susan. Bench introduced them to Janie.

"Why don't you follow us? If you want to wait for Bench to take you home, you can hang out with us. We haven't had lunch. Have you?"

"No. Sorry, I don't think I can eat. I have so much energy I need to burn it off."

"Ah, a girl after my own heart. I'm a trainer, and we have this amazing gym down the block. You need to see it. Bench, can you pick her up from there?"

"You're sure it's not a problem?" Janie asked before Bench could answer.

"Are you kidding? I love showing off my gym. Besides, you may decide you want to take some self-defense classes," Susan suggested.

"I wouldn't mind having some butt kicking skills," Janie replied.

"Let's go then."

Bench watched as the girls left, wondering if Avery would fit in just as quickly as Janie had.

CHAPTER 22

Ethan had the group relocate to the war room. After everyone settled in, Ethan began his questioning.

"Turbo, what do you have for us?"

"I knew about the NDA, it's in Avery's cloud storage. I don't have her laptop, but anything stored remotely in her cloud, I have access to."

"We have the laptop, but our techs haven't found anything yet," Cruz stated.

"Want to let us dig around it? Turbo, how long would it take for you to search it?"

"I'd just copy the hard drive and give the laptop back. Actually, if you don't want the evidence to leave your office, I just need the IP address for the laptop to have remote access. Your team doesn't even have to know I've been in there. It won't impact your evidence either, since I'm simply copying existing files and not altering the originals."

Cruz mulled it over and Dax agreed, they needed to have another set of eyes on the data.

"Fine. I'll have my tech person send it to me and I'll forward you the IP address. Chain of custody shouldn't be an issue, but I'll have them download the hard drive just in case someone claims it's been manipulated." Cruz took out his cell and sent a quick text. Five minutes later he was forwarding the address to Turbo.

"Give me a second," Turbo said before she left the room. When she returned, she had a laptop she was removing from a box. She began entering the IP address and let it run diagnostics before setting a keyword search.

"Okay, that will do part of the work. Now, as for what I've found. She had several nasty emails from her ex-boyfriend. Janie was right, he is not a nice person. Your tech should be able to recover those... If not, let me know," Turbo told Cruz.

"Anything we should worry about?" Ranger asked.

"Just the typical, 'you ruined my life' crap. He was a douche to her. Gaslighting her and blaming her for everything that had ever gone wrong in his life. He even blamed her for his vanilla sex life. Like I said, a big douche-canoe."

Bench would have to do research on the whole gaslighting thing. He'd heard about it, but never understood it. That would change after this job was over. He had zero tolerance for someone belittling another person. He might just have to sink that douche's canoe.

"Anything about Callum? Was she suspicious of him?" Ethan asked.

"Not that I could find. I saw her contract with him, along with the NDA. I didn't do a deep dive into the document, but it sounds like Janie did. Her notes were all saved. I forwarded those to you while I was getting the laptop, so they should be in your email... Yours too," she said to Dax and Cruz.

"Honestly, there wasn't anything more than what Janie told us. Her parents were dismissal of her job. Her brother doted on her and she loved her nephew. Her ex was an SOB, and the contract with Callum was a financial godsend. She used the first installment to pay her rent six months out. The second installment helped her pay her car off in full. He wasn't cheating her out of money. According to the contract, she had two more installments remaining. She was paid a bonus if the story came in early. As far as an employer, Callum is above board and fair."

"Yeah, none of that is helpful," Ethan replied. "Before I tell you about Ramsey, I'd like to hear from you two. What can you tell us about the copycat killer?"

Bench could feel their eyes on him, so to push this discussion forward he told them to speak freely.

"It's not a pretty story, Bench. Are you sure you want to stay and hear this?" Dax asked.

"I'm sure. I'm assuming this has to do with Hillary."

"It would appear that the copycat picked up where Ramsey left off with Hillary."

"What does that mean?"

"Ramsey's first seven killings were specific. The victims were targeted and stalked. But your wife and son's death were random. We were on site for Avery's first visit with Ramsey. He gave her information that we never knew. He told her his motives for the first seven. When asked about your wife's, he said it was the best kill he'd ever experienced, because he was able to take two lives at once."

Bench hadn't responded, but he clenched his jaw and clenched and unclenched his fists.

"Are you okay, big guy?" Ranger asked him.

"Go on," Bench ordered.

"According to Ramsey, he knew the copycat killer and had told him how euphoric your family's death was. Avery tried to get the name, or even a clue, but he wouldn't answer."

"What were his reasons for the other kills?" Dodger asked.

"He believed they deserved to die because they sinned... Things like adultery, spousal abuse, stealing. Stuff like that," Cruz answered.

"But murder isn't a sin?" Spud asked.

"Apparently not. Anyway, Avery worked her magic and like I said, we gained more intel than we'd ever had before. When she pressed him on the copycat killer, he shut down. He only wanted to talk about his kills, not the others," Cruz continued.

"But he knows who he is. Did you get the impression that he'd been in contact with the killer?" Bench asked.

"I did, and so did Cruz. He was too familiar with the case, but he didn't reveal anything that hadn't been in the news. We've held back a lot on these killings. We learned from Ramsey to not show all our cards."

"What did you hold back, Dax?" Ranger asked his friend.

"This goes no further than this room. The specifics have been contained for those on a need to know basis."

"Of course," Ethan answered for the group.

"The first five victims were pregnant."

Bench dropped his head, letting out a string of curses, then stated the obvious. "Like Hillary."

"Sort of. They were in the early stages, anywhere from six weeks to five months. Each kill increased in the length of her term. So victim number four was four months and five was five."

"Got it," Bench growled.

"The earlier ones wouldn't have been noticeable. I'm assuming their pregnancies were discovered during their autopsies," Ethan stated.

"Yes, but that's not how we knew they were pregnant or that they were linked together," Cruz stated, and then gave the team the gruesome details regarding the pregnancy tests and the simulated surgical skills.

"Is Avery pregnant?" Ethan asked Turbo.

"There's nothing in her files to indicate that she was even seeing anyone. I'll have to pull her medical records to confirm if there's a pregnancy or not."

Dax put his fingers in his ears, rolling his tongue to make the sound of lalalalalala. "Geez, give us a warning when you're going to talk about illegally hacking medical records."

"I'll make sure to do that next time," Turbo chuckled as she continued explaining that by all appearances, Avery was in good health and without child.

"So his MO changed. Does that even make sense?" Ranger asked.

"It's hard to say. Remember, Ramsey changed when he murdered Hillary."

"True, but did you guys ever consider that Ramsey might have had a partner, especially if the new killings are now following a specific pattern? Could it be that Ramsey did the first seven killings, then his partner murdered Hillary? If that's the case, he wouldn't be a copycat, he'd be an accessory."

"We've thought about that, but we just don't have any evidence supporting that theory," Cruz stated.

"Besides, Ramsey confessed to killing Hillary. Now, I'm not saying he's not had contact with the copycat, but it's unreasonable to believe he's orchestrating it from behind bars," Dax stated.

"It wouldn't be the first time," Dodger replied.

"No, it wouldn't. But I know this warden, and he's not someone who would allow this to happen on his watch. He's one of the good ones," Dax vouched.

"So, let me recap and make sure I have everything correct," Bench stated. "Avery went out to try to find someone suspicious. She says her goodbyes to Jane at ten, but never leaves or perhaps returns to the bar. Two hours later, I stopped her from being abducted. Somewhere between the time I dropped her off and she got in her car, either her ex, the copycat killer or someone else took her."

"True," Cruz stated.

"So why aren't you exploring those other two options? Why do you automatically assume she's in the arms of the copycat, especially since it's unlikely she's pregnant?" Dodger asked.

"We have detectives looking at those other two, but it would be shortsighted to not see there's a link between her visiting Ramsey and investigating the copycat, and not assume she's in his scope."

"Dax is right," Bench said. "It makes more sense to assume she's been taken by the copycat killer. Okay, to continue with what I think I understand. Janie is uncomfortable with Callum. Whether it's because of the subject matter Avery is researching, or it's Callum himself, he gives off vibes that make her not trust him."

"True."

"And this copycat killer may or may not have been an accomplice to Ramsey, and may or may not have been my wife's murderer."

"That's correct," Dax confirms.

"Then what's next?" Bench asked the group. "How do we find Avery and find the truth behind Ramsey and his copycat?"

"I'm meeting with Ramsey tomorrow morning," Ethan answered.

"I'm going with you," Bench replied.

"I figured. They're expecting us both."

"I know we didn't settle anything today, but I think we're on the right track. Turbo, I want you to see if there's anything new on Avery's laptop, but I'd like a deep dive into Callum Easton as well. I'm assuming Avery wasn't

Easton's first ghostwriter. Find out who the other ones were. We need to know if the NDAs are consistent. This person should be listed as a researcher in his acknowledgments."

"On it."

"Dodger, can you and Spud take shifts and watch Easton? I'd like twenty-four-hour surveillance."

"Sure thing."

"That would be good. We can't authorize that, especially with nothing to physically link him, with the exception of a dog and a woman's ick radar. Which I'm not minimizing, I'm just saying," Cruz stated.

"We'll reconnect tomorrow after Bench and I come back from Huntsville," Ethan told the group.

"What are you thinking, Bench?" Ranger asked him once Dax and Cruz had left.

"I think Janie's right. There's something off with Callum. It wasn't what he said, or even how he acted... It was just a vibe."

"And the whole dog thing freaks me out," Spud said. "Dogs, especially hunting dogs, are reliable. We may not know what Bailey's normal behavior is, but Janie does. Heck, she even has a spare kennel, so she knows this dog. If it bothered her enough to bring it to our attention, then we need to trust her instincts."

"I agree. When I was with the Rangers, we had a K-9 team. What these dogs can tell you is amazing, but you have to be looking and listening. Never underestimate any clue, whatever it is."

"Not to change the subject, but has anyone heard from Archer?" Dodger asked.

"I need to check in with Axel. I don't have anything to tell them. Maybe I can give them a lead in the fight this week. I'll call Ricardo and find out who's matched to fight. I'll check on Archer while I'm there. They're grooming him to become my handler, which would make our job much easier."

"Just let us know what you need from us, brother. We've got your six," Ranger said as they exited the conference room.

And Bench knew those weren't casual words... They were genuine.

CHAPTER 23

Avery had spent the last three hours searching the house for something. She didn't know what, but surely there had to be something Callum had overlooked. He didn't typically kidnap his victims. He killed and moved on. Avery had no doubt that he was working in an unknown territory himself, which meant he would make mistakes.

But now, she had to admit defeat. She couldn't find anything to use for her escape. If she knew where the cameras were, she'd be able to avoid those areas.

'Cameras! Idiot.'

If she was fascinated with spyware, surely a serial killer would be too. She walked through the house once more, room by room. She located three smoke detectors; the kitchen, the living room, and the bedroom she was staying in. Why would there be one in her bedroom, which wasn't the master, and not in the others? Taking the dining room chair into her bedroom, she struggled, but eventually popped the cover off the detector.

"There you are."

Now she was faced with a decision, a hard one. Should

she leave them, hoping it would keep Callum from returning, or remove them and let the cards fall where they would?

'What would Bench do?'

Who was she kidding? Bench wouldn't have been captured in the first place. He also wouldn't have been stalking a serial killer.

"And he wouldn't be talking to himself while standing on a chair."

What she did know was Bench wouldn't let Callum have the upper hand. He'd confront him head on. Bench wouldn't back down from a fight, and neither would she.

So she took a leap, literally took a leap, because she had to jump in the air to knock the smoke detector off the ceiling. When it crashed to the floor, the camera was aimed directly at her face.

Looking down at it, she smiled right before she lowered her foot on the camera and crushed it under her weight.

"Take that you psychopath!"

She then dragged the chair into the living area and finally the kitchen, ridding the detectors of their monitoring devices. It wasn't until she smashed them to bits did she wonder if the house was being monitored by an outside company. Could she have set off the alarm and seen if the fire department would've shown up? Well, it was too late now.

Avery was sure there were other spyware devices in the house, but knowing she'd done something to get the upper hand over Callum was the hope she needed. She walked into the master bedroom and the en suite bathroom. She shut off the water valve under the sink and kicked at the pipe. She kept kicking, but it wouldn't budge. The house was old enough to still have metal pipes. They would make fabulous weapons, only if she could disconnect them.

She switched legs and continued to beat against the pipe.

The force was shooting pain up her legs and into her hip bone.

'Take a break. At least now I have a plan starting to form.'

Avery closed the cabinet and made sure there was no evidence of her poor attempt before she went into the kitchen, and came face to face with a very pissed off Callum.

"Guess you found the cameras. Or at least three of them."

"I'll keep looking. If you thought I'd just sit around and write your stupid book, then you're even crazier than I thought you were."

"I bet you spent hours trying to find a way of connecting with the outside world. You see, Avery, my researchers are good at gathering a lot of information that might never make it into the final book. One of those was how to make sure someone could not contact 911 with a laptop. You can thank Kelli for that, or you could if she'd lived. Oh well, such is life... no pun intended."

"You didn't need to bet. You were spying on me all day. You obviously heard my frustration."

"True. I especially liked how you figured I would monitor your keystrokes. I hadn't expected you to do a hard reset, but it was pretty interesting. You really are resourceful. We could've made a good team."

"You mean, if you didn't have to kill me."

"Something like that. Ironically, I probably wouldn't have had to, until you discovered Kelli was having an affair. I blame Ramsey for that. He fed you too much information, but that's why he's there and I'm here."

"Did you think I'd link Kelli with you? How?"

"Don't worry, when I discovered how, I corrected it. Kelli no longer has any ties to me."

"But you still made the decision to kill me."

"I had to be sure. You're too smart for your own good. Really, it's a compliment to you."

"Geez, thanks!" After holding her tongue for as long as she could, she asked about his wife.

"Does she know who you really are? What you really are?"

"If I actually had a wife, then probably not. I'd never marry someone smarter than me, except on paper of course."

"Wait, you're not married? Your bio says you've been married for twelve years."

"You should know that fiction is stranger than life. No, Avery, I'm not married, nor do I ever want to be married. You really shouldn't believe everything you read. That's an author's first mistake."

"Reading?"

"No, reading what others write. Never read a review. They're either paid reviews to blow smoke up your shorts, or they're trolls who get a small satisfaction out of their lives by leaving one-star reviews. A true fan, reads. The review is when she shares it with a friend, and so on and so forth. The others are meant to drive up your ad sales, your placement and exposure. But as we both know, not all exposure is good."

"If only I'd have the time to benefit from your pearls of wisdom," Avery sneered. She had wanted to learn from him. She had been excited when she thought she'd get to work with a true master, someone who could open doors for her. All Callum had done was close them... permanently.

"I brought you something to eat. As much as I wanted to stay with you this evening, I need to go home. Your friend, Phelan, met with me and Janie. I need to make sure I stay away from here as much as possible. Once I know I'm not being watched, I'll come back, and we'll get to making that baby."

Ignoring his taunt, she asked about Janie.

"She's a beautiful woman. We might have gotten to know each other a little better, but the meathead showed up. Do you think there's any brains behind all that muscle? I'm not so sure. He didn't have a lot to say to me." After a long pause, Callum asked her, "Nothing? You don't have anything to say?"

"Nothing you'd want to hear."

"Try me."

"It's just funny that you're cockblocked by a meathead. Ironic, really."

"This is new. You're witty. It really is too bad you'll have to die. I think we could've been friends."

"I have friends who are lawyers, accountants, and even a stripper, but I have no desire to have a serial killer as a friend."

Callum didn't respond to her sarcastic remark, instead he handed her a hamburger takeout bag before going back into the garage. He'd finally left... at least for the night.

'I'll take all the wins I can get.'

Ethan and Bench stopped talking when the door opened and Ramsey shuffled into the room.

"You brought company, Bench. Is he going to talk for you this time?"

"Sit down," Bench ordered.

Ramsey however stopped and shook his head in disbelief. "You speak. For two years you've been coming to see me and you've never said one word. What changed?"

"Sit," Bench repeated.

After Ramsey took his seat across from his guests, he rubbed his hands in eager anticipation. "This is going to be good. I can't wait to hear what you have to say."

"Avery Grey," Ethan stated.

Ramsey looked from Ethan to Bench and then back to Ethan, grinning.

"You're involved with Ms. Grey? Well, isn't this a small world."

"Avery Grey is missing, and we believe it has to do with you and the copycat killer," Ethan continued. The two had decided to let Ethan take the lead. If Bench showed any emotion with regards to Avery, Ramsey would clam up.

"Well, since I'm here and accounted for every day, then it's obviously not me. As much as I'd love to have a conjugal visit with Ms. Avery, it wasn't meant to be."

"No, your friend has her."

"What friend would that be? As you already know, I never entertain anymore. Most of my friends have forgotten about me. You know the saying, out of sight, out of mind."

"That's interesting, because we believe your friend has kept in touch with you. Granted not in the ways that most people stay connected, but where there's a will there's a way."

"And how would that be?"

"Through the prison library."

Ramsey tossed his head back in a loud chuckle. "You think I'm getting coded messages from the librarian?"

"No, from the books you've checked out. At this moment, the warden is tossing your cage and confiscating your books. Do you know what we're going to find?"

"Words on a page."

"Words on a page for you."

"Could you get any more vague?"

"Words from Callum Easton, detailing how he has continued the murdering spree that you two started together."

"The author your girlfriend was working with? Really, that's what you think? An author who's too lazy to write his own books is sending me notes in books he hasn't written. If anything, that would mean his ghostwriter was the killer."

Bench's smile caused Ramsey to reconsider his last comments. What had he said that made Bench happy?

"What?" He finally demanded.

"How did you know Callum used a ghostwriter?" Ethan asked.

"Avery told me. That's how she introduced herself."

"Try again. She recorded your interview, and a Texas Ranger and FBI agent were observing from the other side. She never said she was hired as a ghostwriter. In fact, had she, she would've been in breach of her contract with Callum. So let's try again. How did you know Callum used a ghostwriter?"

"I don't know. Maybe it's in his book somewhere."

"Not likely. That's why they're called ghosts. Why would he advertise that he didn't write his own books?"

"Well, it still doesn't change the fact that I wouldn't know what this author was saying, since it wouldn't be his own words."

A brief knock kept Ramsey from continuing his argument. The guard brought in several books by Callum Easton, and one by a self-published author, Lee Callum.

"You know we purchased an eBook version of these books. The problem with eBooks is that it can be edited and reposted in minutes, meaning the old version is no longer in circulation. The same can't be said for hard copies and paperbacks. Once edits are made, the author can purchase all the previous versions and destroy them... That is, unless he's already given some away." Ethan handed the book over to Bench, who flipped to the back, found what he was looking for and violently slammed the book on the metal table. He leaned forward, letting his grin return.

The movement caused Ramsey to jump. As Bench leaned in, Ramsey backed away.

"Do you want to share with us what has made you so happy, Bench?" Ethan asked.

"Researcher, Kelli Owens. She was the River Walk Strangler's third victim."

It had been hard to identify Bench's tone. It was a mixture of 'gotcha' and 'you lose.'

"So here's what we think happened. You and Callum worked together in killing the first seven victims. Then Hillary caught your eye. Now this is where it gets a little convoluted. If we're to believe that Callum continued with his killing spree, then Hillary's death was the pivotal reason for the change in the MO. So we're guessing you didn't kill Hillary... Callum did. You've been trying to rile up Bench here, when in fact you're just an imposter. You weren't twisted enough to take an unborn child. I mean, really think about it... You were trying to adhere to a moral compass with the first seven. You believed their deaths were justified. It was Callum who changed the balance when he killed Hillary."

"That's not true. I killed her and the baby." Looking at Bench, he slammed his hand against the table, "I killed them! Not Callum! It was me!"

Bench took that opportunity to stand up and nod to the guard. Ethan began to follow him out when Ramsey yelled, "It was me. Callum is a pansy. He started over with the girls because I told him how orgasmic it was to kill your wife and cut your child out. That was me!" he continued to yell.

Ethan put his hand on Bench's shoulder and continued their exit out of the room. Once they'd cleared the door, Bench held himself up against the wall with his hands braced against his thighs. He struggled to get air in his lungs. As much as Ethan wanted to console Bench, he knew he needed space. Ethan couldn't imagine the level of control Bench had to keep himself from killing Ramsey. He wanted to, and it wasn't even personal for Ethan.

"Come on, Bench. Let's go get Avery back."

Bench immediately stood straight, resigned to save Avery from the fate Hillary had suffered.

'I can't lose her too.'

* * *

Bench listened while Ethan updated Cruz on their conversation and the notation in the first edition.

"We have the book, and as you requested, the warden gave us a video clip of the meeting. While it won't change Ramsey's sentence, it does give us confirmation that he worked with Callum. I'll have Turbo send you the file. It's in my cloud so she can access it."

"We haven't found Callum yet. We lost track of him after he left ECP yesterday. He didn't return to his house. We're trying to find any other properties that he might own."

"Get Turbo to help you. Between all of our resources, we should be able to find him."

"Will do. How's Bench?" Cruz asked.

"About as well as can be expected. You'll see what I mean when you watch the video. It was tough."

"Let him know we're going to find his girl."

Laughing, Ethan looked over at Bench who had heard the conversation and just shook his head.

"He heard you. Talk soon."

"She's not my girl. I don't even know her. Besides, I'm not ready to move on."

"Let me tell you a story..."

CHAPTER 25

Callum had only been gone a couple of hours before he returned, and this time there was no levity or sarcasm. He was angry. What had changed? He was supposed to stay close to his house to fool the police.

"This is your fault!" He yelled and threw a vase against the wall.

"What are you talking about?" Avery asked as she skirted the broken vase.

"Your friends at ECP are staking out my house. MY HOUSE. Why would they be suspicious? It was that dog. It had to be. I didn't give anything away."

"What about Bailey? Did you hurt her?"

Callum threw back his head and roared. "I would have if your friend hadn't picked her up first. Then Phelan showed up unexpectedly. I should've taken them both out right then and there."

Avery was the one that wanted to roar with laughter. Callum take out Bench? Not even on Bench's worst day could she ever see that happening. But what did Bailey have to do with this madness?

Avery didn't want to enrage Callum any more, so she held back from asking any questions. If she could shirk into the background, she'd feel a little safer. In his frenzy, he might decide to rape or murder her... Neither were ideal.

'I'll take door number three, please.'

She could hear Callum yelling and throwing things around the house. She'd made herself as small as possible, not letting him think she was a threat because truth be told, she wasn't. She didn't have any martial arts or ninja moves, no weapon training, and no visible means of escape. She had tons of useless facts in her head, one too many binge-watching weekends, and a strong desire to live. She would have to work with what she had, and worry about what she didn't later.

The way Callum was going on, she wondered if her rescue was in the making. Would he kill her and make a run for it, or would he stand his ground, determined to complete his mission? What had happened when he met with ECP? Did Bench see through his façade? She sure hadn't, which was inexcusable. After everything Jeffery had put her through, she vowed to be more aware of how others acted. She hadn't wanted to be blindsided again. So how did she miss it? Was the lure of money and a foot in the door enough to blind her from seeing the man behind the name? Was she star-struck? Callum was a local and well-renowned author. Or was it a combination of all of the above? Avery never considered herself to be a shallow person, but if Callum's fame, contacts and money had diluted her senses and dulled any warning signs, then she was destined to be fooled by people, especially men, for the rest of her life. For however long that was.

'But what about Bench?'

Well now, he brought up all kinds of questions. Questions she'd been asking herself since their kiss. It didn't seem sufficient to call it simply a kiss. It was more, at least to her. It felt like he was sucking her soul out of her body and exchanging it with a portion of his own. What would it feel like to have someone like him in her life? Would he be too alpha? It was one thing to be an alpha in bed, but not in life. She didn't want a controlling man. Been there... done that. So, could a man like Bench relinquish control? Could he let her be her own person, and not a shell that he controlled and manipulated? Was he too much man for her to handle? Let's face it, even if he was, she wanted to try and get a handhold on him.

'And why are you daydreaming about one, when the other wants to kill you?'

"It won't matter if you're dead," she scolded herself quietly.

CHAPTER 26

"Status," Ethan demanded. He and Bench had spent the three-hour drive back to San Antonio making several plans. Of course, without knowing where Avery was being kept or even if she was still alive, their plans were fluid.

"I couldn't find any property under Callum Easton. I also looked under his pen name. Then I started wondering if Callum Easton could also be a pen name, and it was. His legal name is Lyle Isaac Dixon. I have four properties, one of which is in the hill country. Dodger and Spud are already heading that way," Turbo replied.

"Where's the other three?" Bench asked.

"Houston, Lubbock, and Lake Charles, Louisiana."

"All of those cities are within a five-hour road trip," Ranger stated. "I can call my contact at HPD and have him do a wellness check at the Houston location. It'd save us time from going there."

"Good idea. What about Lubbock and Lake Charles? Do any of you have contacts out that way you can reach out to?" Ethan asked the group.

"My brother is a detective with the New Orleans PD. It

would take too long for him to go there, but I'm sure he has contacts he could call on for assistance," Bench replied.

"Great. That leaves us with Lubbock," Ethan said.

"I can help with that," Cruz interrupted. "We have an FBI office there. They can call the local PD for assistance if needed."

"That would be great. Everyone go and make your calls, and we'll wait to hear back from Spud and Dodger."

"John, it's me. I need a favor…" Bench said to his brother as he left the conference room.

* * *

"The house looks dark. There are no signs of life, but the location would be perfect for a safehouse. It's nestled on a few acres, and at least ten miles from the city," Dodger relayed to the team through his cell phone.

"Also, the nearest neighbor is probably three or four miles away," Spud added.

"Turbo, can you get us some satellite images?" Ethan asked.

"On it."

"How close can you get to the house without detection?" Bench questioned.

"If there aren't any countermeasures, we can walk right up to the front door. It's the unknowns that have held us back. We haven't seen cameras, but that doesn't mean there aren't any," Dodger stated.

"I think it's worth the risk," Spud added. "The sooner we can cross this off as a possible location, the better."

"Agreed. Stay on the line and do your recon," Ethan instructed.

The four in the conference room waited as they heard

Dodger and Spud exit the truck to get their surveillance up and running.

"Okay, we're sending in a drone. The blinds are all closed and there's sun-blocking curtains up, so we can't see through the windows," Dodger informed the team.

"Wait, look at that," Spud replied.

"What is it?" Bench nearly yelled over the speaker. Ethan looked over at him and reminded him they were trying to keep the noise level down. "Sorry."

"Okay, there's wiring around the window. It's most likely live explosives. You might want to give the other locations a heads up," Spud stated.

"On it," Ranger said as he walked out of the room, calling each of their contacts with an update.

"Here's the images," Turbo said as she sync'd her computer with the overhead projector.

"And here's the infrared," she said and clicked over to the next image. "Crap on a cracker!"

"Dodger and Spud. The grounds are highly rigged. I'm glad you used the drone. You guys could've tripped one of those mines."

"Guys, watch your steps," Ethan ordered. "Turbo, get the infrareds to Ranger so he can share them with the other three teams."

Turbo shot the images over to Spud and Dodger's cells before sending Ranger the other location's files they would need.

Bench stood and walked outside the conference room, giving Ranger an update on the property and possible explosives rigged to the windows, and most likely doors.

Ranger quickly alerted the teams of the possible threats and forwarded the images to their contacts.

Bench entered the room just as Dodger was asking for further instructions.

"I'm going to meet you there," Bench answered.

"Bench," Ethan started to object.

"No, Ethan. I have to go. I can get there in forty-five minutes. I can't just sit here and listen to everyone giving updates. I have to be there."

Ethan nodded, understanding all too well how impossible it was to sit around and not take the lead in getting his woman back. Hadn't Ethan just jumped in the line of fire for Kensley? And he'd do it again… Without any hesitation.

"I can go with you," Ranger offered.

"No, three operatives should be enough. Besides, you need to continue being the liaison with the other law enforcement officers."

Bench pulled out his Baretta, checked the clip and then went to the armory for additional weapons, including smoke bombs. His last stop was to his locker where he collected his knives.

When he ran smack into Turbo, she reminded him that he needed to get some Kevlar vests for everyone.

"Thanks!"

"Someday you're going to have to tell me why you prefer using knives," she said.

"I'm surprised you don't already know, little miss hacker."

"Oh, I have my assumptions, but that's all they are."

"I'll tell you later," Bench said as he exited the door, jumped into his truck and peeled out of the parking lot.

* * *

Ranger, Ethan and Turbo remained in the conference room fielding calls and gathering more intel about Lyle.

"You want to hear something bizarre?" Turbo asked.

"Of course," Ranger replied.

"Ramsey's initials spell JAR, and Callum's real name spells out LID. Freaky, right?"

"Yeah, that is," Ethan answered.

"So what do you think the story is behind Bench's fascination with knives?" Ranger asked Turbo. He'd walked up when they had been discussing it.

"I think it's because of his father. He makes custom blades then sells them on eBay and Amazon. Some date back twenty and thirty years, most likely Bench and his brother were part of their making."

"That's a strange habit," Ranger said.

"Not for a former CIA/SOG operative," Ethan explained.

"Really? More acronyms. What is a SOG?" Turbo asked.

"Special Operations Group. Although they're now called SAG, or Special Activities Group."

"Still not helpful."

"Back in Vietnam, the SOG was part of a paramilitary operation, where the various agencies recruited from Delta and SEAL teams."

"So his father was a CIA Special Forces operative?" Turbo asked.

"That would be the easiest way to explain it. All military branches report to the DoD, but the CIA's focus is gathering intel, Special Forces are the door kickers... Those two were merged into the SOG."

"A super soldier. That's way cool. How do you know all of this? I mean, wouldn't he be all Jason Bourne... you know... if I tell you, I'll have to kill you, kind of stuff?" Turbo asked.

"Woman, you need to lay off the romance books and tv shows. Real life is a lot different," Ranger jokingly replied.

"But fiction is so much better than reality. There's always a HEA or HFN."

"Now it's your turn to reveal what those acronyms are," Ethan laughed.

"Happily Ever After or Happy For Now."

"Of course it is." Ranger smirked.

Before Turbo could reply, Ethan answered his ringing phone and motioned to the group to stop the chatter.

"Let me put you on speaker," Ethan stated. "Okay Bench, we're all here."

"My brother just called and said the house was clear. They used the schematics Turbo sent, and it was a good thing they did. The land was littered with traps, not just mines either. They are contacting the local Feds to come and secure the site."

"Perfect. Ranger hasn't heard from the other two yet. What do you see there?"

"Just like the guys said, the house is locked up tight, but I think there's a gap in the security we can take advantage of."

"Go on,"

"As Dodger said, there's a car in the garage. This means the driveway shouldn't have any explosives. That's our only noticeable option."

"Makes sense. Ranger, let the others know," Ethan instructed. "Okay, Ranger's doing that now. Now tell me what you need from us."

"We need to notify Cruz and Dax, as well as the Austin PD. They would be the largest department in the area. They need to be aware of a potential hostage situation, and live explosives."

"On it," Turbo said as she also left the room.

"It's just you and me now. Talk to me, Bench. Where's your head?"

"I'm good. This is just another rescue mission."

"We both know that's not true. You can deny to yourself that there's no attraction or feelings for Avery, but you're just fooling yourself. However, for this mission, you need to stay focused. Callum has already shown us his hand. He's not only a murderer, he's also paranoid. If he wasn't unhinged enough, you've now got a loose cannon to deal with."

"We don't even know that she's alive, or that he's keeping her here or at one of the other houses."

"That's true, but we work with what we have. And what we have is speculations. We will work on the premise that Avery is alive. In what condition, we don't know. When you breach, you need to expect the worst and hope for the best. As far as we know, Callum isn't working with anyone this time around, which means at best you have two in the house. What's the plan?"

"Let me put you on speaker so Dodger and Spud can add their two cents," Bench said.

"Hey, Ethan" Dodger said. "We think Bench's plan to go straight up the driveway and through the garage is a good option. I doubt he uses an electronic opener, it would be too risky with other electronic triggering devices."

"Makes sense. Let us do some research on the risk factors. When are you going to breach?"

"If the other two houses are clear, then I think we should wait until dark, maybe 0100. I'd prefer to minimize him being prepared for us, and I want to avoid a potential hostage situation."

While 0300 was the most optimal time based on a person's REM cycle, this wouldn't have been considered be a hard extraction. Since it was only one tango, opting to go in earlier shouldn't present any problems.

"I agree, Bench. Hang tight, I'll call you with updates within the hour. Let me know if anything else changes."

"Will do."

After they disconnected from Ethan, Dodger suggested a way of spending their wait time.

"Willow downloaded Callum's latest book on my phone.

Want to take a look at it while we wait? It might give us some insight into his thinking."

"We should download all his books published within the last five years," Spud suggested.

"On it." Dodger logged back into his Amazon account and purchased the eBooks.

"Great, while we wait to see if a serial killer is lurking behind closed doors, two hundred feet away, we're going to delve into his thoughts for the cost of seven dollars."

"Knowledge is power," Dodger replied.

"Like my grandma always said, 'a stitch in the time saves nine.'"

The two men groaned at Spud's southern sayings.

"What in the world does that mean?" Dodger inquired.

"Please don't ask... you're just encouraging him," Bench growled.

"It means," Spud said, ignoring Bench. "A little effort now might save you a lot of effort later."

"Just read the words of a psychopath, please."

"Yes, sir... *Bench mad... Bench smash*," Spud said causing the guys to laugh at Bench's words when they were confronting members of the Aryan Nation to find Spud's daughter, Tabbie.

CHAPTER 27

Avery listened as Callum continued throwing things, yelling and cursing, and blaming Bailey. He sounded deranged, and a little desperate.

Then an hour passed without any noises in the house. She could hear him doing something in the garage. She'd wanted to look in there, but wasn't sure if that door had been wired as well. She needed to find another way out, but that required her leaving the safety of her room and risk running into Callum.

First, she needed a plan. She'd gotten a lay of the land before Callum's return. From the hallway, she could see the family room. With the open concept floor plan, she had a clear view of the downstairs, minus the master and her bedroom.

It was the master bath that she'd tried to bust the pipe in, but now that Callum was back, she couldn't risk it again. There was another bathroom upstairs, but it most likely had welded lead pipes too. It was time to ditch that option. She wasn't physically able to remove the pipe, and she'd only be exhausting her body for nothing.

Slipping out of her room, she went upstairs hoping to find something, anything that she could use.

In the bathroom, she grabbed the shower curtain rod, a bottle of toilet bowl cleaner with bleach, glass cleaner with ammonia, some liquid hand soap and the trash bin. She removed the rubbing alcohol, peroxide and gauzes and tape from the medicine cabinet.

She left the items in a pile by the stairs, but needed to complete her search and get the stash back to her bedroom. *'Not my bedroom. My prison.'*

A quick search of the remaining bedrooms only turned up empty closets, dust bunnies under the mattresses and a hanging mirror. That she could work with.

She quickly put all the treasures in the closet downstairs. She listened but still heard banging in the garage. What was he making out there? More importantly, did she really want to know?

'Um, no.'

What now? She had all these great finds; bleach, ammonia, and rubbing alcohol, but nothing came to mind. Why is it that you can retain a bunch of useless information when you don't need it and forget how to use it when needed? Like removing stains off her copper pots. Did she need salt or baking soda, or both? Who knew… she sure couldn't remember. And then it hit her. Salt and baking soda are kept in the kitchen. What an idiot! Why hadn't she thought of the cleaning supplies and spices in the cabinets?

She tried to think of all the MythBusters episodes that she'd regularly binge-watched, but was drawing a blank. The items she retrieved could make some kind of weapon… what, she wasn't sure yet.

'Geez, Avery, calm down and think. You've got this!'

She found a plethora of things she could use. She grabbed

the mop bucket, a roll of paper towels, a couple of water bottles, cooking oil and rubber gloves from the pantry.

Then in the spice cabinet, she pulled out cayenne pepper, red crushed pepper, black pepper, chili powder, and some Cajun seasoning.

Then she found the motherload... baking soda and vinegar.

'Oh, bottle bomb, here you come.'

She heard Callum walking in from the garage, so she threw everything in the mop bucket and scurried back into her room.

'That was too close.' She exhaled in relief, pushed the dresser up against the door and took inventory of her stash.

"Alright, I have enough things to make a pepper spray of some sort," she mumbled. She realized she hadn't grabbed a bowl or spoon. She listened as Callum started the shower, and quickly retrieved the items she'd stored in the hall closet and the utensils. She then reset the dresser in place.

"Okay, what else?" She wondered as she put all the pepper spray ingredients to the side, along with some vegetable oil.

If only she had alcohol, she could make a Molotov cocktail. If only...

But she did have items she could use to make a bottle bomb. It wouldn't cause any real damage, but it might give her some kind of diversion.

She pushed those items aside.

That left her with ammonia and bleach, albeit in low dosage, but maybe adding hand soap, and rubbing alcohol would help. A chemist she was not, but she did have common sense. She knew none of these items would maim or kill Callum, but they were something. She would prove she wasn't a victim, nor was she a helpless little woman.

First, the pepper spray. The effects of adding all the

ingredients at once she didn't know. But honestly, what did she have to lose?

"Alright, let's get started."

She needed a bottle, so tentatively she mixed the two cleaners together in the mop bucket. Now she had spray bottles.

In the plastic bowl, she added four heaping teaspoons of each spice. Foolishly she had neglected to cover her face, and was already coughing and had watering eyes. She dug through her suitcase and pulled out a t-shirt, and wrapping it around her nose and mouth. Her eyes, however, were a lost cause. But it proved one thing… The pepper spray was potent.

If she remembered correctly, she needed to add some cooking oil, and rubbing alcohol. Again, it would work or it wouldn't, she'd just have to hope for the best. She covered the soaked spices with a paper towel so they could blend together and strengthen its potency before pouring the solution into the now empty spray bottle.

"Okay, now for the bomb."

It wasn't a true bomb, more like a liquid firecracker, but it would have to do.

Imagine if she'd researched bombs online? The NSA would probably beat her door down thinking she was a terrorist. She giggled as she imagined telling the officers, *'I'm sorry. I'm a writer. This is just research, I promise.'*

She took a huge guzzle of the water before pouring the rest of it into the other empty bottle.

She poured half of the vinegar into the bucket, giving her another empty bottle. To be on the safe side, she only used the remaining half of the vinegar. When mixed with the baking soda, the chemicals would react, sending the bottle off like a rocket. To keep the soda from touching the vinegar, she folded the soda into a paper towel and wedged it into the opening before recapping it. Unfortunately, she wouldn't know if it worked until she shook the bottle. If she remembered correctly, once the vinegar came into contact with the baking soda, she'd have an explosive device she could launch at Callum.

The last thing she had was the bucket with the vinegar, ammonia and bleach. In theory, it should burn his eyes and hopefully disable him enough for her to escape.

She took the rest of the pepper spices and put them in the empty trashcan from the bathroom. She added more oil and rubbing alcohol as well, because why not? She shook the solution carefully until she felt it was mixed sufficiently, or until she started coughing, and then poured some in her last empty spray bottle. Time to test it. In theory she knew they worked independent of each other, but when combined, would they hold their potency or did the oil and alcohol mute their effect? Opening the closet, she sprayed the solution in the corner.

"Yep, it works," she said through her coughing fit, despite having a t-shirt over her face.

Now it was time to figure out how to slow Callum down. The things she'd made would stun him, but not stop him.

Slowly removing the dresser, she could hear the television downstairs. He obviously wasn't concerned with her being a threat if he felt safe enough to watch the sports channel. What a cliché? Violence and sports went together just as well as grilled cheese and tomato soup. Then a light bulb dinged over her head. Canned goods. She needed to get in the kitchen, but with an open concept house, she'd be seen immediately. But that would be a risk she'd have to take, when the time was right.

Now it was time to get her bag ready. She would leave that night. She knew she couldn't exit through the doors or windows, but Callum had entered from the garage. There hadn't been any explosions. Granted he could've disengaged them, but it was her only way out of this nightmare.

According to the oven clock it was nearly midnight. It was go-time. She took the bucket she'd mixed the concoction in, and placed it above the open door to his bedroom. If he went there first, at least she'd have an early warning signal.

Her escape would have to be executed in the right order and at the right time. For once, she was thankful for her organizational skills. Too many times she'd gotten mired in the weeds, trying to focus on one time. Her life was managed with markers, post-it notes, paperclips and a dry erase board. With none of those available, she mentally viewed her timeline and took step one.

"What are you doing?" Callum asked when Avery walked into the kitchen. She'd known he'd say something to her, so she was prepared.

"The burger made my stomach queasy. I'm going to see if there's any chicken noodle soup. As far as I know, you aren't planning on starving me to death."

"Eat whatever you want. I already told you, there's nothing in there that you can use to escape."

"Got it, thanks for the reminder. I can't believe I almost forgot this wasn't a writer's workshop retreat."

"What a mouth you have."

Avery's goal was to keep his defenses lowered. She didn't want him on the offense. Ha! Guess sports analogies were helpful.

She reached into her waistband and removed the pillowcase she'd taken from the bed. As quickly as she could, she eased canned foods into the case. She couldn't get greedy and overload it, she still had to get past Callum without causing too much of a scene. Once the bag was packed, she pushed it inside the pantry, then pulled out a can of soup for him to see. She pulled the lid open leaving her the metal lid. It could be useful, so she pocketed it.

"I'll be back when the soup's ready," Avery told Callum as she exited the room. She hoped this would be enough of a warning so that when she came back, he wouldn't pay her any attention and wouldn't be prepared for an attack.

Dressed in the darkest clothes she had, Avery armed herself with her weapons, the shower rod, and a pair of Callum's tennis shoes and placed them just outside the garage door entrance. She'd have to act quickly. The shoes were going to take too much time to put on, so she'd leave them, hoping he'd trip over his own laces. She'd have to make her escape barefooted. Her only other option were her club heels... but she'd risk a cut foot rather than a broken ankle any day of the week.

Returning to the kitchen, bucket in hand, she removed the soup from the microwave, poured the hot substance in the bleach bucket and retrieved her bag of cans.

It was now or never.

With Callum's back to her, she gathered the pillowcase by the end and swung as hard as she could. The weight was a little distorted, and she hadn't gotten a full-on hit, but it was enough to push him forward onto the floor.

As he stood, ready to attack, she took the bleach bucket, with spices and hot soup and threw it in his face. His yells and curses gave her the ability to lunge for the garage door.

Once she was inside, she wedged the shower rod under the doorknob. It wouldn't stop him, but with the suction cupping the concrete floor, it might provide some resistance.

Now for the true test. Could she open the garage manually? She knew it could be done, but she hadn't seen how on the Discovery channel.

Her only option was to flip the switch on the wall, and hope she didn't blow them both up. Once the door opened enough for her to exit, she heard him breaking through the door into the garage. She shook the bottle bomb and threw it at him. As expected, it caused more smoke than anything else, but it did what it was supposed to do… slow him down.

She'd nearly cleared the garage when her leg was swiped out from underneath her. She couldn't reach her pepper spray, but she could grab the soup ring. Placing the pull tab around her finger, she swiped the edge of the rough metal hard against the arm restraining her. The immediate pain and blood shocked Callum, enough for her to break free and flee the garage.

'I am woman… hear me roar!'

CHAPTER 28

"There! The door just opened." Spud pointed, just as they saw a figure clad in black take off running.

"Is that him?" Dodger asked.

"No clue, but I'm going after whoever it is," Bench said as he sprinted across the yard, skipping over the cluster of leaves they'd earlier placed around the mines for easy recognition.

He was closing in, when the runner stopped, pulled out a spray bottle and shot him full force with a pepper spray solution.

"Seriously?" Bench growled.

"Bench?"

"Avery. Is that you? I can't see... is it you?"

"Oh my God, Bench. I thought you were Callum. I'm sorry." He could hear Avery walking toward him and yelled for her to stop.

"I said I'm sorry," Avery snapped.

"Honey, there's underground mines. How you missed them is a miracle. Do you see a bundle of leaves anywhere near you?"

"Yes, all around me. There's one beside your left foot." She'd been cursing the full moon earlier but now she was thankful for it.

"Alright. I have no way of knowing if these are duds, homemade or military grade, so we'll err on the side of caution. Come hold my hand and direct me around the leaves."

"Okay. What about Callum?"

"Dodger and Spud are inside, they'll get him. Don't worry, he won't ever hurt you or anyone else."

A wave of relief washed over Bench when Avery's fingers intertwined with his.

"He's the copycat killer," Avery said in between giving Bench directions.

"We know. He also worked with Ramsey. I'm sorry it took so long to figure it out. Did he hurt you?"

"No. He had a plan on when he would kill me."

"We'll catch up soon. The FBI and Rangers will be here in thirty or forty-five minutes."

"What the…" Bench heard through Dodger's coms.

"Dodger! What is it? What's wrong?" Bench responded immediately. He pulled Avery to a stop, still trying to blink away the residue from the pepper spray.

"Ask your girl if she boobytrapped the master bedroom."

"Oh, I forgot to tell you. I pulled a Home Alone trick. There was a trashcan above the bedroom door filled with bleach, ammonia, and the pepper spray spices. Tell them to watch out when they open the…"

She wasn't able to finish before Bench heard another round of cursing.

"I think they found it," Bench said, chuckling.

"I'm so sorry! Are they okay?"

"They'll be fine. Spud's a medic, he'll be able to irrigate all the crap you spewed on us."

"Are they still able to get Callum?" Bench could hear the fear in her voice, so he held back his quick retort and answered her truthfully.

"Honey, these guys can still do their job, even through a little bleach, or with a bullet, Avery. Now, let's get in the truck. You take the lead."

As Bench was helping Avery into the truck, Ranger called him.

"Hey, Ranger. We have Avery safe and sound. Callum is being apprehended by Dodger and Spud."

"That's great news. I wanted to tell you guys the mines are altered paintball mines. When one was tripped in Lake Charles, it shot out nails. Everyone was okay, it was triggered by an explosives expert on the bomb squad."

"I'm glad we didn't trip on any of those here. We did encounter a few doses of pepper spray, but thanks for letting us know. We're going to wait for Cruz, and then we're heading back to ECP. Him and Dax will meet us there to interview Avery after Callum is in custody."

"Sounds good. We'll have fresh coffee ready, and I'll go get some kolaches."

"Thanks. Bye."

"Spud," Bench said through his coms. "Heads up, they're paintball mines loaded with nails."

"Good to know. We're staying here until the Feds show up. How's Avery?"

Bench looked over her body, trying to keep his perusal clinical. "She's good. No, better than good. She's perfect."

"Sounds good, Bud. Although I'm sure you weren't talking to me. Later."

Bench took the comm out of his ear and pulled Avery tight against his body.

"You scared me to death," Bench said as he ran his hands

over her hair, down her back, and finally relaxed with her weight pressing against his chest.

"I was too. I thought I was going to die." Avery hadn't cried through the entire ordeal, but now safe and secured in Bench's arms, she let her tears fall freely. Whether it was the freedom she found in Bench's arms or the stench of peppers and bleach that added to her tears, she'd never say.

Bench didn't shush her or minimize her fear. He of all people understood the need to let out stress after a life-altering event. Unfortunately, he'd never let tears flow, instead he'd let his fists strike.

He opened the door and they sat in silence and in each other's clutches until the police lights and sirens approached from down the lane.

It was at that moment Avery knew her nightmare was over, and she was truly safe... Thanks to Bench and his team.

CHAPTER 29

Avery had fallen asleep on their way back to San Antonio. Except for the time that she'd been drugged, she'd not slept in nearly forty-eight hours. Nestled against Bench's body, with his arms securely wrapped around her, she felt at peace... Peaceful enough to fall asleep.

"Avery, honey, we're here," Bench whispered while he gently moved her.

"Oh, sorry. I didn't mean to fall asleep. Where are we?"

"You're at our office... ECP. The FBI and Texas Rangers will meet us here later to conduct your interview. This will give you some time to relax, maybe call your family. We even have a place where you can get some rest while we wait."

"Okay. I would like to clean up."

"Sure, we have showers down in the gym. I think there's some scrubs down there, but I'll make sure. We usually keep some on hand."

"Why?"

"Sometimes when we rescue people, they aren't always dressed. We take scrubs and hospital gowns for those that are injured or naked."

"Rescue people? Is that what you do?"

"Most of the time. We occasionally do bodyguard or protection duty, and even some undercover work, but our bread and butter comes from hostage retrieval."

"That's very noble, Bench. I knew you were a good guy."

"I don't know how you'd know that. I've ignored you, threatened you, and kissed you. Noble wouldn't be the first word I'd expect to hear. My mother would've taken a switch after me for how I've treated you."

"You didn't mistreat me. And for the record, I stalked you, argued with you, and if I remember correctly, I kissed you right back."

"Oh, I remember. Lord, do I remember. I hope we do that again, soon."

"You do?"

"I do. Now let's get you set up in the gym's locker room. You can shower, use the steam room, or just wash up. Do you need anything before I leave you alone?"

"Um, I think I'll be okay. Callum brought some clothes from my apartment, so I have clean clothes on, but, well..."

"What?"

"Can I have some socks or maybe some booties?"

Bench looked down at her bare feet.

"Are you hurt? You should have told me. I would've carried you."

"They're okay, nothing more than a few scrapes. I was going to take a pair of his shoes, but it would've taken too much time to put them on. Besides, I'd rather walk around barefoot than put my feet in his sneakers."

"I'll find you something. Gennifer and Kensley live right upstairs. They might even have something you can wear. I'll check with them."

"But I don't know them."

"They're our owners' wife and girlfriend. Gennifer also works with ECP as a pilot."

"Wow! Y'all have a pilot?"

"A couple, actually. Now go wash up. We'll talk after you've had some rest. I'll send the ladies down with some goodies in a bit."

"Thank you, Bench. For everything. I…" Avery couldn't finish because of the emotions threatening to overtake her. It was as if her adrenaline had finally crashed.

"Hey," Bench said as he moved into her personal space and wrapped his large arms around her slight frame. She relaxed and let her head rest against his heart. The constant beating eased away some of Avery's tension.

Bench needed to know that she was alright too. With Avery up against his chest, he kissed her temple, letting his lips rest a little longer than he should have. Before he did anything stupid, he pulled back and broke their cocoon of comfort.

"Now go do your thing and I'll meet you in the conference room. Either Genni or Kensley can get you where you need to be. I need to go wash off this pepper spray. It is strong."

"Okay." Avery smiled when she heard Bench chuckle.

When Avery was out of sight, he called Genni and asked for her help. He was leaving Avery in capable and loving hands, just not in his. He wouldn't let his emotions and fear override his good thinking. He needed distance. He needed to remember why they met.

"Hillary," he repeated what his brain was saying on repeat. *'Hillary.'*

* * *

Avery had spent nearly three hours detailing her relationship with Callum, her kidnapping, and his confessions. Or as she said, "*him gloating about one-upping the police.*"

"So his plan was for you to be victim number six, but only after he'd impregnated you. Is that right?" Dax asked.

"And when I was six months along, he'd kill me and the baby."

Avery had been thankful that Dax called her brother. Tim had worked with both Dax and Cruz before, and she felt Tim would respond better if the details were delivered from a law enforcement's point of view.

That hadn't stopped him from storming into ECP, demanding to see his sister. Since they were meeting in the private war room, Steve escorted Tim inside.

"Oh my God, Avery! What the…" When Bench stood and blocked his approach to Avery, Tim realized he'd been yelling.

"Sorry," Tim said, relaxing and softening his tone. "Thank God you're okay. We've been worried sick! Have you called Mom and Dad yet?"

Avery walked into her brother's large arms. She hadn't realized how much she appreciated her family until the thought of never seeing them again seemed to be a reality.

"I'm okay. I'll call them as soon as I'm done here. Come on, let's sit. You need to meet the group who saved me."

Avery introduced the ECP team, and Tim greeted Dax and Cruz.

"I can't thank you all enough for rescuing my baby sister."

"We didn't save her… she did all of that by herself," Bench replied.

Dodger then enlightened the group about all the boobytraps Avery had created.

"She got me good with the pepper spray," Bench said and chuckled to everyone's amazement.

When he noticed their expression, he said, "What? It was funny."

"It was, but I wasn't sure you would think so," Ranger stated.

"She got me with an ammonia and bleach concoction," Dodger added.

"Not me," Spud said while raising his hands for everyone to see they were clean and unharmed. "But let me just say Avery, you're mighty resourceful and pretty creative. To make all those traps and set them, all why being held prisoner by a serial killer... Well, I hope my Tabbie grows up to be just like you."

"It wasn't me... not really. Most of it was from TV shows or books I've read. Not my creativity, but thanks anyway."

"You see! I keep telling these men that you can learn a lot from books. They're a great resource... Even romance books," Turbo proudly stated and high fived Avery.

As they began to debate the worthiness of various romance novels, Dax interrupted the two women.

"Tim, we've gotten what we need from Avery. If we need any clarification or have more questions, we can come to her. If you want to take your sister home, she's free to go."

"Absolutely. Avery, you can stay with me and Melissa, or I can take you to Mom and Dad's."

"I just want to go home, Tim. I'm exhausted, and I'll probably fall asleep the minute my head hits the pillow."

"We can talk about it in the car." Tim refrained from arguing in front of the crowd.

"I have no doubt we all will." Avery then asked about her clothing and car.

"We'll get it all back to you as soon as possible. They will still need to be processed for evidence. While we don't think we'll find anything with someone as intelligent as Lyle Dixon, you just never know."

The men had earlier explained that Callum was a pen name, and Lyle was his legal name. However, they all agreed to refer to him as Callum Easton, as everyone was already familiar with the name. So hearing him called Lyle was a little discomforting. She was once again reminded that she wasn't as alert and prepared as she thought she was. She hadn't even known he was using a pen name. *'So stupid.'*

"It's no rush. I just didn't want anyone to forget."

Avery stood and shook everyone's hand, then gave Turbo a hug for all their efforts in finding her. However, when she made her way to Bench, he took her hand. Instead of shaking it, he led her out of the room.

"Hey!" Avery heard her brother call out, followed by Ethan reassuring him she would be okay.

Once they'd cleared the offices, Bench pulled her into the empty break room.

"Look, Avery. I have so much to say to you, starting with I'm sorry."

"Sorry for what?"

"For ignoring your calls, for threatening you legally, and for driving you to the point of getting kidnapped. I should've just swallowed my pride and answered your questions. I shouldn't have left you in the parking lot. It is unforgivable and reckless on my part."

"You big, oaf! My lack of interview with you had absolutely nothing to do with my being kidnapped by Callum. Trust me, that was all my own fault, as was going back into that club alone. Honestly, the closer I got to finding the copycat, the more I made myself a target. And as for the legal stuff, geez, I'd have probably done the same if someone was stalking and harassing me."

"It's just that when Hillary was taken, I couldn't do anything to stop it. I've lived with that guilt for five years. I'd never want you to think I cared so little about your life."

"Come here, you big beautiful man," Avery said as she pulled him into a full-body hug. "You carry too much guilt, Bench," she whispered against the base of his throat. She felt his body coil and then uncoil at her words. Only it wasn't her words that affected him, it was their intimate hold and the warm words whispered against his throat.

Bench rested his chin on the crown of her head, and realized he hadn't held someone so close and intimately in over five years. He missed the contact... the intimacy... the cocoon.

"I'd like to get to know you better."

"You would?" Avery asked.

"Yes, but this is new to me. I can't promise you anything, only that I'll try to let you in."

"I think that's the best offer I've ever heard. Most people keep all the personal things, both good and bad, shielded away from others, including myself. That makes it hard to know the real person. I'll try to let you in as well."

"Good," he growled. She chuckled when the sound reverberated against his chest where she could feel it.

"Are you ready?" Her brother asked, thereby breaking their bubble. Bench, however, didn't let her escape his hold. He didn't care if her brother was a Texas Ranger. He could've been the President of the United States, or the Prince of Wales. Either way, he wouldn't let Tim break their connection, not until they were both ready.

"Give me a minute," Avery replied, with her lips resting near Bench's Adam's apple.

"Fine. I'll be outside."

Neither responded to his statement, nor did they pull apart, not until Bench reminded her that she needed rest.

"I'd say you could call me, but I don't have a phone anymore," Avery said as she untwined herself.

"Wait here," he ordered and jogged out of the room.

Seconds later he walked back in, tearing the packaging off a new disposable phone.

"Here, use this. It's not going to give you internet service, but there's a calling card inside the case. It doesn't have a lot of minutes, but it should work for the next couple of days until you get a replacement."

"Are you sure? Don't y'all need like, hundreds of burner phones?"

"And we have twice that many down in the armory. Take it. Here's my phone number," he said, handing her a piece of paper. "Call or text me and let me know you're okay. You aren't in any danger, but our brains don't always use logic."

"I will. Thank you, Bench. I mean it. Not just for coming to my rescue, but for this," she said, moving her index finger back and forth between them.

"You don't have to thank me for this," he chuckled as he mimicked her finger movement.

Avery stood on her tiptoes and placed a soft kiss on his lips. As much as he wanted to take control and kiss her with all the passion he was developing, he knew the time wasn't right.

Instead, he interlaced their fingers and escorted her out to her brother's dually pickup. The truck's height gave him all the permission he needed to lift her up and buckle her seatbelt.

"I'll call you," she promised before he shut the door and waved goodbye.

As they pulled out of the parking lot, Tim assessed his sister before commenting. "Well, he's a lot different from Jeffery. I'm in favor of this one."

"You and me both," Avery said as she innocently traced the outline of her lips.

'So do I.'

CHAPTER 30

Avery laid wide awake, staring at the ceiling. She'd finally convinced her family that she could sleep at her own home. Tim had driven her straight to their parent's house, and Melissa met him there in her Jeep. After a tight hug, Melissa handed over the keys to her car.

"Take it until you get yours back. You need transportation."

Janie had offered to come and stay the night with her, but Avery insisted she was fine. She had to be fine. She had no logical reason not to be...

...Fine.

But staring at her ceiling confirmed what she'd been denying... She wasn't fine.

It was too late to call anyone, so she made herself a cup of mint tea with a splash of Texas Bourbon. While it was soothing, it wasn't enough.

She turned the tv on, but nothing interested her. She even pulled out an old econ textbook, that was a sure-fire way of falling asleep. She'd done it plenty of times while in college.

But did it help? Not to sleep. Instead, she had to get up and balance her checkbook.

So when her cell phone dinged with a message, she jumped. The notification broke the eerie silence suffocating her.

Her immediate fear was Callum had escaped and was looking for her. Then her brain cells began firing. No one knew the cell number, unless she'd personally given it to them. Then, what serial killer would send a text to their potential victim?

"Don't be an idiot!" She swiped and saw that the message was from Bench.

"Are you asleep? If you're still awake, call me."

Touching his phone number from the text, she waited for Bench's voice to calm her nerves.

"Hey," he said, all gruff and sleepy sounding.

"What's wrong? Did something happen? Did Callum escape?"

"Oh, no, Avery. Nothing like that. I'm sorry, babe. I didn't mean to scare you. I was worried about you. Thank you for texting and letting me know you were home safely."

"Oh, okay, and you're welcome," she said, dragging out the okay to sound like OooKaaa.

"I don't know why I texted you. I've always had a tough time turning my brain off after a mission or a fight. It's like my body is exhausted, but my mind is stuck on overdrive."

"I understand. I'm so tired, but I can't sleep. I've tried everything. Maybe I should've stayed with Tim. I... I'm not comfortable here. Callum had been here and packed up clothes for me. He was in my dresser, touching my unmentionables. Just the thought gives me the heebie jeebies."

"Maybe you should stay with someone. Do you need a ride?"

"I have my sister-in-law's jeep, but I'm afraid to walk to my parking spot. What if someone tries to take me again?"

"I can come get you, if you want."

"Thanks, but you've already done enough."

"Hey, we're not keeping score."

Avery giggled. "It's a good thing because I'd be the loser."

"Nah. Let's call it even."

"That must be some modern math there. You've saved me twice from Callum, and the first time I wasn't too thankful."

"Even-Steven."

Avery remained silent until Bench prompted her to ask her questions. He understood her need for answers. He got understood her.

"Can you tell me what happened after I left the office?"

"Nothing much, really. At least not on our side. The Feds will have to go back and look at the previous murders to see if Callum and Ramsey really worked together. They're also going to put information in VICAP and see if any other victims match."

"Will there be any DNA to match?"

"I'm not sure. There's still a lot of details law enforcement is keeping close to their chest."

"Do you know one hundred percent that Callum is behind bars?"

"Yes. Dodger and Spud kept him restrained until Cruz arrived. Apparently, you did quite a number on him. Spud said he had chemical burns, a rough looking incision on his right arm, and a bump the size of a goose egg on his head. You'll have to tell me about that later."

"I had to do whatever I could to get away. But now, I can't believe I did it. He could've killed me right then, had he been able to stop me. I could be dead right now."

"But you aren't. Cruz read him his rights and charged him with five counts of murder, kidnapping, and attempted murder. Of course, that number could change, but he's not getting away."

"He'll probably try to represent himself. He believes he's smarter than everyone else, including legal counsel."

"Let's hope he does. Only a stupid man hires himself as his lawyer," Bench stated.

"Or an egotistical idiot."

"True. Now, how do I get you to sleep?"

"I don't know."

"I have some suggestions. Do you want to hear them?"

"Sure."

"First, I could pick you up and take you to your family. Second, I pick you up and take you to Janie's. Third, I pick you up and bring you back to my place, and you sleep in the spare bedroom. Fourth, I go and sleep on your couch, so you can relax. Or five, we continue talking until you fall asleep on me."

"Um, well, number three sounds like trouble in the making and I've had about all the trouble I can handle this week. Number four sounds fantastic, except I have the most uncomfortable couch ever made. So, number five is probably the safest and more realistic choice."

"Then let's get started. Are you in bed right now?"

"Yes."

"Are you laying down or reclining?"

"Reclining."

"Then lay back and relax. Burrow down in your blankets. Put the phone on speaker and rest it on the mattress by your head. Tell me when you're done."

"…Done."

"Good. Now, what would you like to talk about?"

"Can I ask you anything?"

"Yes, but there may be some things I can't answer because of military clearance or ECP missions. Things about Hillary, well, the answers may take me a little longer to respond, but I'll talk to you about her and our life together."

"Thank you, Bench, but I'm not ready for any deep conversations. Tell me about your childhood."

So he did. Bench hadn't talked about his family or his past to anyone since Hillary's death. He'd completely shut down, but he found he enjoyed talking to Avery. She'd wait while he considered her question, never pressuring him. Instead, she remained patient and silent.

"When I was, I don't know, maybe eight or nine, my father took me and my brother to his workshop. We'd never been allowed in there, and there was a large padlock on the door. I can't tell you how many times Johnny and I tried to pick that stupid lock."

"At eight years old?"

"We were probably five or six at the time. John's two years younger, so he pretty much just tagged along at that age."

"So what was in the shed?"

"Don't ever let my dad hear you call his pride and joy a shed."

"Got it," she giggled.

"At the time, I didn't know how cool my father was... To me he was just Dad. But when he let us into his workshop, my eyes were opened. There were knives everywhere. There wasn't one spot on the workbench that wasn't covered. He had hunting knives, scalpel-type blades, and ninja stars."

"I would've been terrified as an eight-year-old to be near so many sharp objects."

"That's pretty much how my mom felt. She wanted us to play with green army men, not become them. She wanted us to use water guns, not assault rifles. But Dad told her that if he taught us how to respect the tools, we'd be safer in the future."

"A tool?"

"Got that, did you now? Yeah, it didn't fly with my mother either. He promised to not let us hold them until we were double digits. Let me tell you, it seemed to take forever to turn ten. The day I did, I woke up and stood by the door waiting for my dad to unlock it. It was like every Christmas and birthday never existed after I was ten."

"I bet you were so cute."

"I don't know about that, but when I turned thirteen, I was able to help him make the knives. And by the time I graduated high school and joined the Army, I was proficient in using just about every type of sword or knife. If it sliced, diced or stabbed, I knew how to use it."

"Do you make them now?"

"Not in a long time. It would've been better than joining a fight club, but since Hillary died, I've not done much of anything except work and fight. I want to change that... starting today."

"Today?" She asked while yawning.

"You're getting sleepy."

"No, I'm listening," she denied.

"Just close your eyes and listen to my voice."

"I like your voice. It fits you."

"How so?"

Avery yawned again, and then answered his question. "Tough and manly, but also smooth and sexy. You should do audiobooks. I bet women would be downloading all your recordings."

"Would you?"

"Every single one, even if you were reading documentaries or nonfiction."

"That's some commitment."

"Don't get distracted. You said you were going to start living beginning today."

"For one, I'm opening up to you. I plan on doing that with others too. I need to visit Hillary's family. I need to see my own family. I need to get to know my nieces and nephews. I've been a horrible son, brother and uncle."

"I'm sure they understand."

"They do, but they shouldn't have to. My life changed in one day, and everything blew up. Honestly, I never recovered."

"You can do it."

"You offering to help me?"

"You know I will. Although, I'm not sure what that requires."

"I don't either, but I'd like for us to figure it out together."

"Aren't you scared?" She whispered.

"Down to my bones. It's easy to live in the shadows, to live a solitary life. But I'm determined to get out more, accept some of the invites I continuously decline. I hope to love again, and have a family."

"Really? I figured you wouldn't want children."

"I do. Wesley wasn't expected. We wanted to wait until I could stay stateside... Maybe become an instructor. But the minute I saw the ultrasound, I fell in love. I'll drive my wife crazy – basically shadowing and bubble wrapping her. But if she can handle my paranoid need to protect my family, then I'd like to have several kids."

"A bunch of little Benches running around, begging to play with knives."

"Something like that."

Avery yawned once again, and Bench had an idea.

"Avery, I want you to close your eyes and listen while I read a book that Turbo gave me for my next assignment."

"What is it? A military manual?"

"Just close your eyes and listen..."

Bench opened the paperback book that had a shirtless

man on the cover. He was wearing leather pants, and leaning against a Harley.

'Good grief, I can't believe I'm about to do this.'

"Chapter One – Luna knew walking into the biker bar was not a good decision, but she was without options. Her 2002 Corolla had been like family. No, it had been better than her family, and definitely more reliable. How did her pot smoking, free loving parents raise her to become a computer science nerd. Well, if they knew her side job, there wouldn't be any doubt about her parentage. Moonlighting as a phone sex operator wasn't how she expected to spend her evenings.

'Don't judge. College was expensive, especially when my parents smoked away their paychecks.'

Her poor twenty-year-old car could rest in peace forever after it was towed off the highway.

'Are years for a car like dog years? Is she one hundred and forty?'

"What's up, Doll?" A biker with a beard as long as his chest, shimmied closer than she was comfortable with.

"Oh, sorry. I need to find the tow guy. The police officer said he would be here. Do you know which one he is?"

"Sure, Doll." The nameless biker yelled across the bar for Trigger.

As if the crowd sensed the energy change, the room split, highlighting the most gorgeous man Luna had ever seen. She couldn't have held back her long and loud exhale even if she'd tried. It was as if her lungs needed as much space as they could take.

He openly perused her body, shamelessly studying her legs and slowly assessed her features. It seemed to take a lifetime for him to meet her eyes. His hooded blue eyes locked her in place. She couldn't tell anyone what the biker was saying next to her. Trigger had taken her body's full attention, including her ability to speak.

"You want me."

Trigger didn't ask. It was a statement. And her answer was yes, God did she want him, but instead she regained her motor skills.

"I need my car towed. I was told I could find you here."

"I'm off-duty."

Was his smirk meant to be sexy? Not likely, but it was, possibly even smoldering. Then his words registered.

"Wait! What? I'm sorry... Did you say you're off-duty?"

"I did, Doll."

"Then can you please get on-duty?"

"I think I could get it on for you."

"Ugh! Really? I'm not here to get hit on, I'm here to have someone take care of my baby."

"The car?" An unknown biker asked.

"Yes, her car," Trigger snapped.

"If he's not going to help you, I will," a third biker said as he closed the space between Luna and Trigger.

"Back off, Ace. I've got this," Trigger growled.

The last thing Luna wanted was to be caught in the middle of a bar fight.

"Avery, are you awake?" Bench asked. When there was no response, he continued to read for another hour until he too started to feel drowsy. He left the phone line open, closed the book, and relaxed into a dream where he was straddling a Harley with Avery clinging to his body and her hands caressing his bare chest.

'Turbo will never know about this...' Bench thought to himself before he woke up in a very uncomfortable situation.

CHAPTER 31

Avery awoke with a start. How long had she been asleep? Looking for her phone, she found it next to her pillow, then she remembered. Not the book, but the voice that calmed and soothed her so she could sleep.

"Oh no, it's one in the afternoon!" Avery pushed back the covers and tried to remember why she'd jolted awake. Then she heard it again. Someone was banging on her door.

Walking over and peering through the peephole she saw her parents, Melissa, Tim, and Janie.

"What are y'all doing here?" She asked as the crew entered.

"We wouldn't have to if you answered your phone," her mother said.

"Or your texts," Janie added.

"Or your door," Tim stated flatly.

Avery looked at Melissa, expecting another jab from her.

"What? I told them you were probably sleeping. I'm sure you didn't sleep much while being held by a serial killer."

Did Avery mention how much she loved her sister-in-law? If not, she should.

"I'm sorry, guys. I didn't fall asleep until maybe four o'clock. I didn't hear the phone or the door."

Nor was she going to tell them her phone line was busy all night, automatically sending all her calls to voicemail.

"I told you guys," Melissa gloated. "Get dressed, we're going out for breakfast."

"Lunch," her father grumbled.

"I'm not really up for going out. Really, guys, I'm okay."

"Then why didn't you fall asleep the minute your head hit the pillow, like you promised me last night?" Tim asked. When he wanted to throw his weight around, he made sure to use that law enforcement tone, and those glaring all too knowing eyes.

"I had to unwind. Why don't we get some takeout and eat here?"

Her mother walked into the kitchen, calling out what little ingredients Avery had.

"I would've made something from scratch, but I'm not sure what to do with Ramen noodle soup, a tomato, and some not yet moldy cheese."

"Sounds like spaghetti, college-style," Janie stated, and then high-fived her former roommate.

"Tim, you and your dad go get something to eat. Melissa and I will get her some groceries. Janie, your job is to get her moving."

And that was her mom... taking charge. She would've made the perfect drill sergeant.

'Who are you kidding? She already was our drill sergeant.'

Once everyone was out of the apartment, Janie pulled Avery down onto her horrible couch.

"Spill it!"

"What? You already know everything about Callum."

"Not that sicko... I'm talking about the strong, silent and gorgeous man that got between you and your brother when he felt you were being verbally attacked. You know, the one who pushed you up against the truck and kissed the daylights out of you. I still can't believe that happened…and you didn't tell me immediately."

"Oh, him," Avery chuckled. "Wait, how do you know about that? It happened right before I was taken."

"Oh, their hacker showed me the video from outside the building. It was grainy, but I saw enough to know what happened. It looked H.O.T. Hot!"

"It was. I promise to give you all the deets, but I have got to shower, have some coffee, and brush my teeth first."

"Fine, go on. I'll make the coffee."

* * *

Janie sat across from Avery and dissected every word, starting with the kiss. It felt too pedestrian to call it a kiss. It was a soul-bearing experience. But Avery didn't know how to explain something like that. If only she knew how to express her words… like a writer.

"What does he mean when he said he wanted to try?"

"I guess he wants to date me."

"Avie… You need to be sure what his intentions are, not guess. I'm guessing you're the first person he's been interested in since his wife's death. You'd be his rebound date."

"What? No way! It's been over five years."

"But to him, it could be five days, five weeks, or five months since he's wanted to move forward. I'm just saying that you need to have a serious conversation, and not just pillow talk, or a stolen kiss here or there… No matter how hot it was."

"I get it. I'll…"

Her thoughts vanished when her phone rang. *Bench!* She

fumbled for the phone but was immediately disappointed when his name didn't pop up.

"Who is it?"

"I don't know. It's not a number I know."

The blood slowly drained from her face. No way could it have been Callum. He wouldn't call her. She'd been so excited when her dad handed her a new phone with the service already connected. But right now, she wished she still had the burner phone that no one but Bench could call.

Without saying a word, Avery handed the phone over to Janie.

"You've reached Avery Grey's attorney. How may I assist you?"

Avery watched as Janie nodded to what the caller was saying, and looked over at Avery before agreeing.

"Avery, this is Douglas Massey. He's Callum's publisher," Janie informed.

Janie had put the phone on speaker and sat it on the coffee table.

"Hello, this is Avery."

"Good morning, Avery. As I told your attorney, I'm with the publishing house that purchased the rights to Callum Easton's novel. I understand from my conversation with both Callum last week, and the police this morning, that you have the research and a manuscript draft ready."

"I do, yes."

"We would like for you to send those over to us, either electronically or we can have a courier come to you."

"Excuse me, Mr. Massey, this is Janie again. What financial benefit is there for my client to send these over to Tilted Crown Publishing?"

"We presented Callum with an advance, and contractual benchmarks so we can publish the manuscript on time."

"Yes, I understand that. However, your contract is with

Mr. Easton, not my client. Legally, she's not obligated to hand those notes over to anyone other than Mr. Easton. Avery met all the requirements outlined in her contract, up until he kidnapped and planned to murder her. So again, those intellectual documents remain in Avery's control. Now, if you'd like to meet next week to discuss moving forward, both with the novel and potential movie rights, I'll be happy to make that happen. How would you like to proceed?"

"Yes, of course. How about Tuesday at eleven? We can go out to lunch after we've come to an amicable agreement."

"Sounds good, and if you'd fax or email me the documents prior to our arrival, I'd appreciate it. Oh, and we'll expect lunch even if we don't reach an amicable agreement."

Avery could hear Mr. Massey chuckle before they continued exchanging contact information. A contract to write a novel, and possible movie rights. What the heck had Janie got her into?

"Well, it looks like you'll have a job starting next week," Janie said with excitement and a shoulder bump.

"It's crazy. I need to wrap my head around this. Too many things are happening all at once."

"Enjoy the ride, Avery. You deserve it."

Over a late lunch, Avery brought her family up to speed, both on the publisher's call and her interest in Bench.

"He seems protective," Tim said.

"He's gorgeous," Melissa added.

"How would you know that?" Tim growled.

"He's thoughtful," her mother added.

"He's broken," her father stated.

"Dad!" Avery gasped at her father's assessment.

"It's the truth. You can't go through what he has and not break. But what is broken can usually be fixed, if given enough time. Just don't rush. You both need to heal. The difference is your healing is just from a few days, his is from years."

Janie nodded and added, "Sometimes something broken can become something even more beautiful when it's put back together again."

Avery had a lot to think about, but for the moment, she relished being with her family. She'd think about Bench tomorrow.

CHAPTER 32

"You're wrong, Avery. You are not a rebound, you're my second chance at love. You're the one that can make me whole once again."

"Don't you see, Bench? I need you whole, all on your own. I can be your other half, your better half, but we both need to be strong, with and without each other. We need to be able to stand alone before we can stand together."

Bench still remembered his reaction to Avery's words six months earlier. He'd argued he was ready to move on, but she had been correct. He needed to start living on his own, truly living, before he could offer her his whole heart.

When he asked how long, she didn't give him any timeframe.

"When you're ready, you'll know. You'll just know."

Should she have been surprised that after a month, he declared he was ready? Or three months? Now it was six months later and he still feared she'd reject him.

What made him think six months would make a difference?

'Because you are ready. You truly believe it. You're not the same

217

person who had to walk away from her. You're better, so much better.' Bench reassured himself.

When Avery walked into the restaurant, his body began to restructure itself. His breathing became shallow, his chest slowed its rising and falling, and his heart pleaded to be one with hers.

'Am I a poet now?'

He'd write all the sonnets in the world if it meant her becoming his. But instead of making a fool out of himself, he rose from the table and went to greet her. The months had done her well. She'd moved into Archer's apartment since he'd relocated to the motorcycle clubhouse. It worried Bench when he saw the fatigue and strain his friend was living through. They all hoped this assignment was nearly over. Each day on the job, Archer lost a part of his soul. Regardless of the outcome, Bench knew Archer needed it to end.

"You look beautiful," Bench told Avery as he pulled out her chair. His impulse was to place a light kiss on her bare shoulder, but he restrained his desires.

"You look good too." The smile she had for him was genuine. It reminded him of that smile all those months ago that drove him to physically react... to taste those lips... to feel her body against his.

"How's the book tour going?" Bench asked to readjust where his thoughts were going.

Not shockingly, Avery's novel became an instant bestseller. The movie studios were fighting for the rights to make an adaptation.

"Exhausting. I'm glad to be home."

"I am too. When do you have to leave again?"

"It's just starting. My schedule is packed for the next four weeks. After that, I don't know. I wished they'd just take one interview and broadcast it on every channel. It's always the same questions, and it's the same answers every time. Do they think I'm going to give them spoilers? Anyway, enough about me. Tell me how you're doing."

"Like you, the job is wearing on me. Archer and I are hopeful that it will wrap up in a few weeks."

Avery didn't know all the details, but she knew Archer and Bench were undercover with a motorcycle club. She worried every day that he or Archer would be outed. But so far they'd been accepted by the club, and even brought into some of their confidences.

"Have you found the mole?"

"We know who she is, but not why she's still undercover. She was the one who finally made contact with Archer. That's really all I can say about Skylar. The Diablos, the Alaskan MC, took their revenge by taking out our club's enforcer. This equalized the balance in their world."

"I don't understand why you guys are still there then. You know the mole, and the Alaska guys have left."

"Our mission changed when we discovered some business we hadn't known was happening in our city."

"Shady business, I'd assume."

"The shadiest. We're trying to figure a way to transition this to ALIAS, since it's their area of expertise. That may be where Skylar will be the most helpful. But let's not talk about my job."

"Or mine."

"Then what would you like to talk about?"

"Us," Avery said with confidence.

"You think I'm ready now?"

"What do you think?"

Bench was prepared for this discussion, but it was still hard. He'd never been comfortable talking about himself, and especially not his feelings. But for Avery, he'd do his best.

"I now understand why you wanted us to wait. I've spent

the last six months facing my demons. I've visited with Hillary's family, even told them about you."

"Really? How did that go?"

"To quote my former sister-in-law, *'It's about time, bonehead.'*"

"They're okay with you moving on?"

"Yes, not that it would've changed my feelings, but my in-laws talked about Hillary in daily conversation. They embraced their pain, and didn't let it paralyze them... Not like me. I should've gone sooner."

"You weren't ready."

"True. I also went and stayed a week with my family. My mother spoiled me. My father and I spent time in his workshop, creating a beautiful blade with an elk's antler."

"What about your nieces and nephews?"

"They're all nearly grown now." Chuckling then, he continued. "Matthew is nine. He's already waiting for his tenth birthday. Apparently, we do become our parents... or at least my brother has."

They continued to talk about his family vacation and when he'd brought the subject to a close, he reached across the table and held her hand.

"Avery, I want us. Not because I need you, which I do, but because I love you. And don't freak out, because I've thought a lot about this. We've talked on the phone a handful of times, but never anything serious. We've gone about our lives, but for me, you've always been in my heart and mind. I've openly talked about Hillary and you and the similarities, but also what makes you unique to me. Those are good things. It made me realize that I have a type."

"Oh, really?" Avery had seen pictures of Hillary, and they were about as far apart in looks as any two people could be.

"Yes. I prefer strong-willed, overly opinionated, independent to a fault and a self-reliant women. You don't need me. You're a strong person. Geez, you saved yourself from a serial killer. But while you may not need me, I need you. I need your strength. I need to hear your opinions, and then your arguments for why I'm wrong."

Avery chuckled. "Because you usually are."

Bench lifted her hand and kissed her knuckles.

"We have a relationship that's not based on lust, but something deeper. So, I'm officially asking you, Miss Avery Grey, New York Times bestseller, and the keeper of my heart, if you'd finally agree to be my girlfriend."

Avery's free hand was wiping away the tears attempting to cling to her lashes.

"I will."

Bench let out a sigh that could have blown every candle out in the restaurant.

"Thank God."

"I just have one question."

"What's that? I'll tell you anything," Bench reassured.

"Your place or mine?"

Avery shrieked, then laughed as Bench pulled her up by their intertwined hands.

"Mine," he growled, as he half dragged, half carried his girlfriend for the first of many pillow talks in their future.

EPILOGUE

Three months later:

Bench, Avery, Archer and Janie sat in the bar listening to the country singer croon. It wasn't Bench or Archer's preferred music, but if Avery wanted to two-step, he'd do it. Him and Archer had been taking lessons with Doc and Felicity. The men weren't concerned with learning the dance moves, or they wouldn't have been if Liam and Spud would shut up. Ironically, both were excellent dancers. Bench knew this because they continually showed Archer and him up.

"Do you want to dance?" Bench asked as he extended his hand.

"Why, thank you kind sir," Avery giggled and accepted his hand.

The slow two-step let Avery rest her head against his chest, relaxing with each breath Bench took.

"What do you want to do tonight?"

Bench watched as Avery bit the bottom of her lip. He noticed she did this whenever she was unsure what his reaction would be to a request.

"Out with it, woman."

"Fine… I was thinking you could read book two in that series Turbo gave me."

"Admit it. It was the sex scenes, wasn't it?"

"I told you that you should do audiobooks. Your husky voice joined with the erotic words, well, yeah, it turned me on."

"I think I can do that. It seems like I remember you moaning when I read the shower scene. Or maybe it was when Trigger threw Luna's legs over his shoulder, or could it have been the time he stopped the bike, and had her reverse cowgirl."

"Yes, Bench, it was all of those. Can we please go home, NOW?"

Bench would never admit how thankful he was that Turbo had given him the books. As much as it was inaccurate regarding motorcycle gangs, he had to admit the sex scenes were straight out of a porn film.

Bench didn't answer her question, he simply pushed her off the dance floor, threw a couple of twenties on the table and left Archer chuckling and Janie clapping.

Archer and Janie had become fast friends. Neither was interested in anything physical, they were content with being each other's partner in crime.

"I didn't think they'd ever go," Janie said after she watched her best friend leave the bar with her man in tow.

"They have it bad."

"No truer words have ever been said. Now, I'm not sure about you, but I'm ready to go. I have a case I need to prepare for, and this place is grating on my last nerve."

"Thank you, Jesus. Come on," Archer said as he helped Janie out of the building. Ever since Avery's abduction, the men made sure to walk the women to their cars, checked the backseat, and left only after she'd safely driven away. Some lessons had to be learned the hard way.

The one good thing to come from the MC undercover job was purchasing a bike. The freedom it provided was worth the added expense. Even though ECP offered to reimburse him, Archer wanted to keep it after the job ended. Maybe he'd take it on a long trip, maybe to Alabama.

Archer hadn't heard or seen the threat, but he felt the bullet rip through his skin. Skidding over the asphalt was nearly as painful as the unprovoked bullet.

* * *

Archer tried to rest after his stint in the hospital. The doctors said the bullet barely missed his lungs. Thankfully, it was a through and through, and would heal eventually. He'd spent ten long months on his assignment and would've leapt for joy, if that had even been possible in his condition, when ALIAS took over the job. Their area of expertise was taking down threats by any means necessary. Not for the first time, he was glad he didn't work for a company who only dealt with human trafficking. He'd take hostage retrieval any day of the week. Radar, the punk, would be dealt with by the club's new enforcer, but it gave him the out he needed. Archer told Axel and their President that he didn't want to be involved in a club where its prospects felt empowered enough to try and assassinate their fellow members. He was done! Fortunately they understood, and Radar's fate was no longer his concern. For the time being, Bench kept in contact with the club connections. As they didn't expect him to leave ECP, there really hadn't been any reason for Bench to drop his cover, which wasn't even a cover... It was just him, the good, the bad, and the ugly. Ethan thought having the club under their purview could be beneficial in the long run.

Grunting, Archer flipped through his mail. He'd not heard from Charlie in months. Even though he'd been undercover, Avery had sublet his apartment and held his mail for him until Bench could hand it over.

His letters to Charlie were his lifeline. He'd told his friend all about the mission, the depravity in the motorcycle club, and their decision for the job to be transferred over to people more equipped to handle the threat lurking in San Antonio. Since he'd returned home, he had two letters from Charlie. The first one was damaged and the post office had secured it in a storage zip-lock baggie.

Opening the first letter, he began reading his friend's words.

"Archer,

I hope you are doing okay. I know you're undercover right now, so if I don't hear back from you I understand.

So here's what's happening over here. My fiery granddaughter is making quite a stir, not that this should surprise you. We'd been approached by a large developer several times who wants to purchase our land. Their first offers were competitive for those that wanted to sell, but as the months went on, the more aggressive they became. Instead of increasing their offers, our friends were paid ten cents on the dollar for their property. Now it's just us holding out. This land has been in my family for nearly a hundred years. It's our home. I can't judge my neighbors for selling out. Most of the original families have either died or sold off years before, and the new owners aren't emotionally tied to the land like I am.

Leenie has pulled out my rifle more times than not, and ran the trespassers off our property. I'm scared she's going to get hurt with her hardheadedness. *(I'm not hard headed... I'm just always right. And I hate bullies.)*"

Archer loved reading Leenie's side comments. For

months, Charlie has had to rely on his granddaughter to type or write the letters. Not to be muted or ignored, Leenie added her own commentary.

"I'm sure she just wrote something that counters my opinions, that's just how she is. If you want one piece of advice to live by… never marry a redhead. Her grandmother, God rest her soul, was just as onry as my Leenie.

Anyway, back to what I was saying. The temperature over here is coming to a boil. I'm not physically able to stand my ground anymore, *(which is why I'm here.)*

You know, when a man reaches my age, has given everything he has to his country, been faithful to a good woman, and raised a rebel *(that's me)*, he should be able to rest knowing his home is safe. Isn't that what we fought for? So citizens would have the freedom to live as they so desired.

Anyway, enough belly-aching. I'm still waiting for you to come visit us over in the true south. Leenie keeps using those sayings you wrote, the ones your buddy says, to liven up the mood here. Really Archer, who can't help himself from chuckling when someone says it's colder than a well-digger's butt? Who touches a man's butt to check the temperature? Well, there's probably some who would volunteer for that job, but not me, *(me either… ugh gross)*.

I don't want to keep you and I know you're a busy man, but remember your friends back in Alabama *(especially when we kick your UT butt! Roll Tide, baby… Roll Tide!!!!!!)*

Take care,
Charlie"

Archer had been concerned over the last couple of letters and the pressure those developers were placing on the octogenarian. They'd bonded years before while they were both recovering stateside at a VA hospital. Charlie had been a boot camp Sergeant for years and never expected to be shot in the back and become wheelchair bound.

But it happened. Charlie recalled the day there was an active shooter on the base, and how he tried to usher his men out of the line of fire. However the coward shot Charlie in the back, leaving him permanently paralyzed. Over the years, the two had become closer, talking about their families, their service, and their future plans. Truth be told, he was the only person Archer confided in.

Charlie reminded Archer on numerous occasions that being a Marine was the best decision he'd ever made.

He hated that his friend was being targeted by big business, but what could he do? Not only did he live four states away, but he wasn't a financier either.

Ripping over the next letter, he noticed it was handwritten, and that the writing was feminine.

"Archer,

This is Leenie. I hate to deliver this news to you through a letter, but I didn't know how else to find you.

The development company has gotten even dirtier with their attacks. At first it was minor irritations, broken fences, salt in my ATV, you know, high school pranks. Then, last month, they brought in these goons that look like they'd come from the Sopranos. They became more aggressive with their attacks. Cattle were brutally slaughtered, and some ranch hands were threatened to leave or face their fists. As of right now, we've lost fifty-percent of our staff. Those staying have nothing to lose (their words not mine.)

But today, they went too far. My grandfather was home alone. I was out with our limited staff, trying to fix fences, counting cattle, and a lot of grunt work.

Anyway, back to Gramps. They pushed their way into our house and physically threatened my grandfather. When I finally got home, he was lying on the floor, his wheelchair was toppled and moved several feet away. Of course he wouldn't tell me who did it, but it didn't take a lot of brain power to figure it out. Now I need to hire someone to stay with him full-time so I can take care of the ranch and not worry about his health. Only he's a stubborn old cuss. He's refused any help that I've tried to hire… so I'm asking for a favor.

My Gramps counts you as one of his closest friends. You've been immortalized in his eyes, so I was hoping that when your assignment ends, could you come for a visit, and maybe stay by his side for a bit? I just need to have enough time to harvest our fields, get the cattle to market, and hire new help for the planting.

I hate to ask for your help, but you'd really be helping my grandfather. Please let me know if this is something you can do."

Archer checked the date on the envelope; it was posted two weeks earlier. As he went to put the letter back in the envelope, another note fell out.

"Archer,

You don't know me, but I work for Charlie and Leenie. I know they've mentioned how bad the conditions here are, but it's so much worse than you've been told.

Last week, Charlie had a heart attack because of all the stress. He's holding his own, but he's in his eighties.

Then today, I came to the homestead for dinner and the house had been ransacked. There was blood smeared around the door jamb that resembled someone trying to fight off being kidnapped. Leenie is missing. The local PD, well, they aren't the most trustworthy, and have been in the developer's pocket for some time. They've turned a blind eye to their attacks, their bullying, and the property damage they've caused.

We need your help. No, Charlie and Leenie need your help. I don't think Charlie's heart will take it if he finds out Leenie is missing. Please call me at the number below if you are able to come.

Thank you,

Alfred Manning"

Archer growled as he made a quick move for his jeans. Charlie needed him. He couldn't lay in bed knowing Leenie was missing for at least two weeks. That was too long to not know what was happening.

Grabbing his cell off the table, he called Ethan.

"I'm heading to Alabama tomorrow. I have something to take care of."

"Is everything alright? Shouldn't you be resting?"

"My friend is in trouble. I've got to go, Ethan. I can't stay here and not help them."

"Do you need our help?"

"I won't know until I get there."

"Okay, let us know if you do. Oh, and Archer?"

"Yeah?"

"Tell Charlie I said hello." Ethan was chuckling as he disconnected the call.

'When will these boys learn nothing gets past me?'

While tossing his clothes into his duffle bag he called Alfred. There was still no word from the kidnappers or Leenie. Time was wasting, time she might not have.

"I'm coming Charlie. We will find your granddaughter and make sure these crooks know not to mess with a Marine."

'Stay strong, Leenie. I will find you.'

Dear Readers,

This note will be different than anything I've ever written to my readers. While I do appreciate my editor at Red Line Editing and Adam's exhausting job of reigning in my commas, today's message is personal.

On April 6th my husband of nearly twenty-five years passed away due to COVID complications. Initially, I was going to pull this release, as well as book one in the ALIAS series, Uncovering Ivy, but when they showed up in my inbox from my editor, it felt like I needed to share these stories with my readers. That being said, most likely book two in the ALIAS series will not release this summer as scheduled.

My husband, Garry, was not only the love of my life, but he was my best friend, and a huge cheerleader for my work. He never met someone who he didn't tell about my writing career. He refused to read my books before their release date. He said he didn't want to influence my writing with his comments, so instead he'd read it and then pick out areas he'd like to know more about. It was because of this that I promised to write a five-years later novellas for my series. Since ECP Alpha is complete, I'm hoping to have it ready this fall as a tribute to my husband.

If you've not downloaded Uncovering Ivy, I suggest you do. It will mesh ECP and ALIAS together and give you insight in the assassination company set in Austin, Texas.

Until next time, be safe and love freely.

Annie

BOOKS BY ANNIE MILLER

ECP Series - Team Bravo

Hunting for Zoey

Hunting for Tabbie

Hunting for Susan

Hunting for Kensley

Hunting for Avery

Hunting for Charlie

ECP Series - Team Alpha:

Securing Willow

Crash Landing

Poison Ivy

Unravel

Black Hat

Securing Lola

Protecting Kallista

Bullets & Lace Wedding Novella

ALIAS PROTECTION

Uncovering Ivy

Uncovering Seven

Uncovering Voodoo

Uncovering GigaByte

Uncovering Blue

Uncovering Falcon

Uncovering Ghost

Uncovering ALIAS

Stand Alone -

Serendipity

Hope

Destiny

Amazon Vella Serials

A Kiss in the Dark

Children & Coloring

The Princess's Friend - Fully Illustrated Children's book

Bella's Big Adventure - Alaska Coloring Book

FUTURE SERIES:

Knight Owl Securities - (2023)

ECP Series - Team Charlie (2024)

ECP Series - Team Delta (2025)

ABOUT THE AUTHOR

Annie is a prime example of what a city girl does when she moves to the country: write award-winning contemporary romance and dramatic novels. From her first book, Destiny, to her most recent ECP series, she has let her imagination take over and filled countless pages with heartfelt characters. The Texas born author likes to travel, chase her grandkids around the house, and on occasionally have a glass of red wine. Follow her on her journey at www.anniemiller.net

Website: www.anniemiller.net
    Email: booksbyanniemiller@gmail.com
    Facebook: www.facebook.com/booksbyanniemiller
    Instagram: www.instagram.com/booksbyanniemiller/
    Goodreads: www.goodreads.com/Annie_Miller
    TikTok: www.tiktok.com/@BooksbyAnnieMiller

There are many more books in this fan fiction world than listed here, for an up-to-date list go to www.AcesPress.com

You can also visit our Amazon page at: http://www.amazon.com/author/operationalpha

Special Forces: Operation Alpha World
Christie Adams: Charity's Heart
Linzi Baxter: Unlocking Dreams
Misha Blake: Flash
Anna Blakely: Rescuing Gracelynn
Julia Bright: Saving Lorelei
Cara Carnes: Protecting Mari
Kendra Mei Chailyn: Beast
Melissa Kay Clarke: Rescuing Annabeth
Samantha A. Cole: Handling Haven
Lorelei Confer: Protecting Sara
KaLyn Cooper: Spring Unveiled
Janie Crouch: Storm
Jordan Dane: Redemption for Avery
Tarina Deaton: Found in the Lost
Riley Edwards: Protecting Olivia
Dorothy Ewels: Knight's Queen
Lila Ferrari: Protecting Joy
Nicole Flockton: Protecting Maria
Hope Ford: Rescuing Karina
Alexa Gregory: Backdraft
Michele Gwynn: Rescuing Emma
Casey Hagen: Shielding Nebraska
Desiree Holt: Protecting Maddie
Kris Jacen, Be With Me
Jesse Jacobson: Protecting Honor
Rayne Lewis: Justice for Mary

Callie Love & Ann Omasta: Hawaii Hottie
A.M. Mahler: Griffin
Ellie Masters: Sybil's Protector
Trish McCallan: Hero Under Fire
Rachel McNeely: The SEAL's Surprise Baby
KD Michaels: Saving Laura
Olivia Michaels: Protecting Harper
Annie Miller: Securing Willow
Keira Montclair: Wolf and the Wild Scots
MJ Nightingale: Protecting Beauty
Victoria Paige: Reclaiming Izabel
Debra Parmley: Protecting Pippa
Danielle Pays: Defending Sarina
Lainey Reese: Protecting New York
KeKe Renée: Protecting Bria
TL Reeve and Michele Ryan: Extracting Mateo
Deanna L. Rowley: Saving Veronica
Angela Rush: Charlotte
Rose Smith: Saving Satin
Lynne St. James: SEAL's Spitfire
Sarah Stone: Shielding Grace
Jen Talty: Burning Desire
Reina Torres, Rescuing Hi'ilani
Savvi V: Loving Lex
LJ Vickery: Circus Comes to Town
Rachel Young: Because of Marissa
R. C. Wynne: Shadows Renewed

Delta Team Three Series
Lori Ryan: Nori's Delta
Becca Jameson: Destiny's Delta
Lynne St James, Gwen's Delta
Elle James: Ivy's Delta
Riley Edwards: Hope's Delta

Police and Fire: Operation Alpha World

Freya Barker: Burning for Autumn
B.P. Beth: Scott
Jane Blythe: Salvaging Marigold
Julia Bright, Justice for Amber
Hadley Finn: Exton
Emily Gray: Shelter for Allegra
Alexa Gregory: Backdraft
Deanndra Hall: Shelter for Sharla
India Kells: Shadow Killer
CM Steele: Guarding Hope
Reina Torres: Justice for Sloane
Aubree Valentine, Justice for Danielle
Maddie Wade: Finding English
Laine Vess: Justice for Lauren

Tarpley VFD Series

Silver James, Fighting for Elena
Deanndra Hall, Fighting for Carly
Haven Rose, Fighting for Calliope
MJ Nightingale, Fighting for Jemma
TL Reeve, Fighting for Brittney
Nicole Flockton, Fighting for Nadia

As you know, this book included at least one character from Susan Stoker's books. To check out more, see below.

SEAL Team Hawaii Series
Finding Elodie
Finding Lexie
Finding Kenna
Finding Monica
Finding Carly (Oct 2022)
Finding Ashlyn (Feb 2023)
Finding Jodelle (July 2023)

Eagle Point Search & Rescue
Searching for Lilly
Searching for Elsie (Jun 2022)
Searching for Bristol (Nov 2022)
Searching for Caryn (April 2023)
Searching for Finley (TBA)
Searching for Heather (TBA)
Searching for Khloe (TBA)

The Refuge Series
Deserving Alaska (Aug 2022)
Deserving Henley (Jan 2023)
Deserving Reese (TBA)
Deserving Cora (TBA)
Deserving Lara (TBA)
Deserving Maisy (TBA)
Deserving Ryleigh (TBA)

Delta Team Two Series
Shielding Gillian
Shielding Kinley

Shielding Aspen
Shielding Jayme (novella)
Shielding Riley
Shielding Devyn
Shielding Ember
Shielding Sierra

SEAL of Protection: Legacy Series

Securing Caite (FREE!)
Securing Brenae (novella)
Securing Sidney
Securing Piper
Securing Zoey
Securing Avery
Securing Kalee
Securing Jane

Delta Force Heroes Series

Rescuing Rayne (FREE!)
Rescuing Aimee (novella)
Rescuing Emily
Rescuing Harley
Marrying Emily (novella)
Rescuing Kassie
Rescuing Bryn
Rescuing Casey
Rescuing Sadie (novella)
Rescuing Wendy
Rescuing Mary
Rescuing Macie (novella)
Rescuing Annie

Badge of Honor: Texas Heroes Series

Justice for Mackenzie (FREE!)

Justice for Mickie
Justice for Corrie
Justice for Laine (novella)
Shelter for Elizabeth
Justice for Boone
Shelter for Adeline
Shelter for Sophie
Justice for Erin
Justice for Milena
Shelter for Blythe
Justice for Hope
Shelter for Quinn
Shelter for Koren
Shelter for Penelope

SEAL of Protection Series
Protecting Caroline (FREE!)
Protecting Alabama
Protecting Fiona
Marrying Caroline (novella)
Protecting Summer
Protecting Cheyenne
Protecting Jessyka
Protecting Julie (novella)
Protecting Melody
Protecting the Future
Protecting Kiera (novella)
Protecting Alabama's Kids (novella)
Protecting Dakota

New York Times, USA Today and *Wall Street Journal* Bestselling Author Susan Stoker has a heart as big as the state of Tennessee where she lives, but this all American girl has also spent the last fourteen years living in Missouri, California,

Colorado, Indiana, and Texas. She's married to a retired Army man who now gets to follow *her* around the country.

www.stokeraces.com
www.AcesPress.com
susan@stokeraces.com

Made in United States
North Haven, CT
22 May 2022

19411674R00143